Helltown Marshal

Clay Jackman – nicknamed The Gunner – was chain light-ning with a Colt .45, maybe the fastest of them all. And so he was hired to tame the wild Texan herd-drivers threatening to turn Chisum into a shooting gallery.

It was their most violent playground of all between Red River and the Rio Grande but Jackman believed he could do it, even if Chisum had its doubters. He wouldn't know for sure until the final gun fell silent and a whole trailtown either lived or died.

Helltown Marshal

Matt James

A Black Horse Western

ROBERT HALE · LONDON

ISBN-10: 0-7090-8022-0
ISBN-13: 978-0-7090-8022-0

Robert Hale Limited
Clerkenwell House
Clerkenwell Green
London EC1R 0HT

Typeset by
Derek Doyle & Associates, Shaw Heath
Printed and bound in Great Britain by
Antony Rowe Limited, Wiltshire

CHAPTER 1

TRAINLOAD OF TROUBLE

The sheriff of Chisum had sat in Midge Griddle's eatery with a mug of coffee going cold before him for longer than he knew, listening to the sounds of trouble building further along the block.

From time to time the errant waves of sound coming from the street would fade some, even die away altogether. Each time this happened he felt a surge of hope that the Texans might not carry out their threat to try and break pard Billy Ringo out of the lock-up – Sheriff Latigo's sturdy lock-up on Main. But each time there was a lull, somebody yelled or cursed and that would set off the angry sounds again.

'More coffee, Sheriff?'

He glanced up at the pretty waitress and shook his head with sudden emphasis. No. No more coffee and no more indefensible delay. He had a job to do and he

5

would damn well do it!

He headed along the back-street at a half-run, trying to ignore the unsteadiness inside. At forty-five the sheriff of Chisum wasn't much for running any more, or dealing with a bunch of drunken Texan cow-herders either, for that matter. But he was still the law, the Texans the lawless, and if he could just reach the jail-house ahead of them and grab down his old faithful sawed-off shotgun, they would realize Chisum wasn't the weak-kneed wide place in the trail they seemed to think it was.

The lawman made it to his office but didn't get to the shotgun. When he came trotting and puffing out to the street from the narrow flanking alley, he realized instantly that it had begun. Red-faced waddies in big hats and spurs were crowding the jailhouse veranda grappling with his deputies, and even as he propped and stared, there came a great cheer and a big-nosed Texan with a five-day growth emerged triumphantly with the lock-up keys in one hand and clutching the shoulder of the grinning prisoner with the other.

At least the sheriff plucked up enough courage to remonstrate with the mob. But a blind man could see he wasn't having any effect and wouldn't have. The trail-riders were even laughing and skylarking as they escorted their cowboy pard across the street for the saloon, with shocked towners looking on from the plankwalks, and only one stern and red-faced senior citizen having the courage to protest as the bunch surged by.

'You've gone too far, Texans!' bawled the mayor, waving his silver-topped cane. 'You'll regret this, and that is a promise, not a threat!'

Jeers greeted his outburst and a flunkey tugged at the mayor's coat-sleeve, fearful for his safety. The mayor allowed himself to be led off to the corner, but when he halted there was no sign that his outrage had abated any.

'That does it, George,' he panted, swabbing at his sweaty face with a spotted kerchief. 'They are forcing our hand, and by glory this time the council will go through with it!'

'What . . . what are you fixin' to do, Mayor Sands?'

'What I promised to do at the last council meeting when we made contingency plans to cover any future trouble these hellions might bring to our town.'

'And what was that, boss?'

'We're going to send for the Gunner, is what!'

For the fifth time during the afternoon run from Clinton to Dodge City, the train grated to a stop.

Clay Jackman opened one eye and looked at the brown land beyond his window, at the plains and low hills which had moved by for hours, sometimes swiftly, sometimes with treacle slowness, but fortunately always shifting him steadily towards his destination.

'Cattle on the tracks agin,' informed the passenger seated opposite, as if he couldn't see this for himself.

Jackman did not reply. The passenger was plainly curious about him and had made several attempts to engage him in conversation since drawing out of Crockett depot, but without success. The marshal was not a sociable man at the best of times, while the challenge awaiting him in Chisum down along the

Oklahoma border at the end of this journey certainly did not fall into the best of anything category, or at least not on paper.

There was an added element to his sombre mood that day. The train journey, with the hot glare coming off the dry land and the grit and dust blowing in was causing some trouble with his eyes, and that always made him testy.

He had drops in his vest pocket prescribed by the druggist back in Elwood. He also had two pairs of wire-rimmed spectacles in the satchel in the luggage rack above, one prescription pair for distance vision and smoked glasses for the glare.

But whoever heard of a 'fast gun peace officer' who wore spectacles?

A lithe cowboy rode into view to hustle the stock off the tracks and the westbound began to pick up speed again. Through the open window Jackman's gaze locked momentarily with the rider. The man was tall, gaunt-ribbed and wild looking. A Texan if he were any judge. Most likely a Texan with chips on both shoulders who was still fighting the War Between the States in his mind. His attention switched to his fellow passengers, most of whom slumped in weary silence while a few either snored or complained in plaintive voices. The discomfort of the journey plainly preoccupied them, and there was ironic speculation on just how much yellow dust they might get to swallow before getting to slake their thirsts on the booming bustling streets of far distant Dodge City.

Jackman would be debarking before Dodge at Plainsville, from where he would stage south-east to the border and Chisum where the mayor, sheriff and town board would doubtless be waiting nervously for their first glimpse of the man responsible for inspiring the headline which had dominated the front page of the *Border Herald* one week earlier:

SEND FOR THE GUNNER!

Jackman's jaw tightened as he closed his eyes again and rested his head against the leather.

He could have done without that splash of publicity and the accompanying critical article comparing the board's new appointment unflatteringly with Hickok, the Earps and Bat Masterson. 'The Gunner' was a tag originally hung on him by his enemies, which he always resented when it was voiced by people who should know better. It suggested that Marshal Clay Jackman was some kind of gunman wearing a badge, whereas he saw himself as a dedicated, professional peace officer who resorted to the gun only when other methods failed.

As he allowed himself to drift off into a light doze he had no intimation of just how close he was at that moment to being called upon to demonstrate those very skills by which he had earned his grim nickname . . . yet again.

It was not the grind of brakes or shouting of cowboys shifting their market-bound herds off the right of way which aroused him this time, but rather the sudden jarring blast of guns, the swift stutter of hoofs and the alarmed cries of his fellow-passengers.

His eyes snapped open. For a moment everything

was blurred and fuzzy round the edges, as was mostly the case when coming out of sleep these days.

Then he saw everybody crowding the windows on the southern side. A woman ducked and held her child close when a six-gun bellowed. Instantly the marshal was heaving his six feet two erect and tugging down the jacket lapels. What the hell was going on here?

It didn't take long to find out.

There was a bunch of seven wild riders galloping abreast of car number three of the westbound, men with a common wild look about them, with their big hats, low-slung gunrigs, looped riatas hanging from saddle horns and, most prominent of all, Colts in hand as their hard-ridden ponies kept pace with the Titan loco, four cars and caboose.

Texans!

Jackman could identify the breed on sight. In Kansas they acted as though they had been the victors in the Civil War, a conflict still being fought in the minds of many of a certain breed of citizen from the Lone Star State.

Then he heard the hairy redhead bellow between gunshots: 'Where is he? Is that woolly-headed wonder town-tamer on board, or was it just a terrible rumour we heard that he was on his way to clean us Texicans out? Marshal, are you in there or did you show yeller again like we expected?'

Jackman stood isolated and remote in the centre of the swaying car as he watched a rider towards the rear reaching for the grab rail of the observation car, leaning recklessly half-out of his big double-girthed Texas-Spanish saddle. The town tamer was travelling incognito, so his fellow passengers had no notion that he was the man the riders were seeking. But he felt that a certain redhead and his pards would have made it their business to find out exactly what he looked like – and the coldness settling inside him was hard as tempered steel.

Damn them!

Each time he was hired to deal with this breed he had acquitted himself in such a punishing manner that only a fool, or bunch of fools, could fail to take the lesson to heart.

Certainly he was taking up an assignment in a place where Texans were the problem, and thanks to trash journalism as promoted by the *Border Herald*, his appointment was now widely publicized.

Plainly this bunch felt they had good reason to react against his coming to Kansas again to impose his personal brand of law upon them, yet he still fiercely resented their actions.

This was lawlessness, and Marshal Jackman had never tolerated that in Missouri, Oklahoma, the Dakotas or Colorado, nor would he do so here.

The rear door of the car burst open and a curly-headed heller came swinging in, pistol in hand and flashing a big grin as people began to panic.

'Hey, it's all right, folks – relax. We ain't a-lookin' to hurt nobody, jest want to see iffen that world champeen Texas-hater is ridin' this li'l old train, is all.' He propped in the centre of the aisle. 'Is there any ten-foot-tall feller what answers to the name of the Gunner aboard this here—'

'I am Marshal Jackman!'

Suddenly every eye was focused on the tall figure in the plain brown suit and hat, standing spraddle-legged in the centre aisle. The Texan blinked then jumped back with his left hand clasped to his heart, eyes popping wide, feigning terror.

'By God and by glory, it is him. Who said we'd find him hidin' under somebody's petticoats?' His .45 bellowed and the bullet slammed into the floor. 'Hey, boys!' he roared. 'He's here right enough, and he looks even scarier and more cussed than we was led to believe.'

Answering howls from without were punctuated by gunblasts and the riders were closing towards the observation platform to clamber aboard as Jackman spoke again.

'Put that weapon away, cowboy!'

'The hell I will!'

With no sign of a grin showing now, the cowboy jerked the pistol in his hand up to firing-level, with hostility blazing in his wild stare. Jackman's right hand blurred and came up with a heavy black gun which exploded in the confined space like a cannon, causing a small child to scream in terror.

The cowboy staggered backwards, slowly, haltingly, all colour gone from his face, the hand clasped still to the ribby chest, desperately trying to stem the dark tide of blood rushing from his body and bubbling round his fingers.

He suddenly crashed to his back with a great clatter just as the next wild man of the Brazos came lunging through the car door with a gun in either fist and murder in his eyes.

12

Jackman triggered again and the man fell backwards through the doorway and dropped from sight. By this time the car was filled with screaming as Jackman stood as implacable as God waiting for the others to make their play.

The Texans who'd made it on to the train's observation platform hesitated uncertainly as though suddenly realizing their danger. Jackman drilled a hole into the car ceiling with his Thuer and shouted for them to discard their weapons. But a wild-eyed redhead hurled his lithe frame though the doorway, eyes blazing with 'border fever'.

That was a Kansan name for the malaise which seemed to afflict Texan drovers when they crossed the territorial line into Kansas with their herds. It manifested itself in resentment of all things 'Northern' – and many had shown themselves ever-ready to seek the cure-all with hot lead.

The plan to jump the Gunner's train had been Redhead's. He could not back water now. He jerked trigger with a snarl and Jackman's return shot instantly smashed his gun arm.

It also effectively destroyed the troublemakers' nerve, for Redhead was their vaunted top gun.

There was a sudden clattering rush for the observation platform with one ashen-faced waddy grabbing Redhead by his good arm and hauling him out after them. The car rocked as two shots slammed from Jackman's gun into the roof above the cowboys' heads, with the result that by the time Jackman stepped out on to the platform it was empty, nothing left behind but a dropped sixshooter and bloodstains.

His lip curled as he leaned out to look back and saw them scattered at intervals along the right of way, tumbling agonizingly down the blue metal rails.

The *Border Herald* and other papers would make much of the fact that the peace officer nicknamed the Gunner had killed one hell-raising Texan and seriously wounded two more.

None of which would affect the tall man who boarded a southbound stage out of Plainsville later that night. It was many years since Marshal Clay Jackman had demonstrated any hint of vulnerability to either words or bullets. Some contended he had made himself harder and faster than any man had a right to be, and maybe they were right.

But even if that were so, the marshal would not be losing any sleep over it. He was a renowned hard man, which was one reason why the Chisum City Board had hired him. They wanted a strong man to stand against the Texans who were continually bringing both their vast herds and their North-hating ways through their town. And after hearing what had happened aboard the 1.30 from Crockett to Plainsville, the gentlemen who had hired him would be convinced they had got exactly what they were paying for.

'Go for your gun, you scum-sucking crackerhead. I ain't killed a Jayhawker all day and that just ain't natural!'

'You first, brush-jumper. The day I can't give a busted-luck Texican a full head start then blow his guts out before he even touches iron, I'll give the game away!'

They stood fifty feet apart on the moonlit street of

Sneak Creek on the Panhandle border, two youthful gunpackers with hooked hands fanning over Colt handles with a hundred eyes watching, yet not a soul on this street.

They'd scared everyone in town indoors.

These gunthrowers from the Pecos were so mean and scary that it seemed they were ready to turn on one another when they couldn't entice any Sneak Creekers to take them on!

What did they feed them on down South to make them so ornery?

Mac Tunney appeared to grow impatient as he continued to crouch there, slim-hipped and snakelike in tight-fitting rig with his face shadowed by a yellow hat.

'Ain't aiming to wait all night, sucker!' he jeered.

'You are dead meat,' responded Olan Quill, and went into his draw.

Tunney responded and Colts glittered like live things as hidden onlookers braced themselves for the thunderous reports, which didn't come. All they heard, all there was to hear, was the rapid dry-fire click of gun hammers on empty chambers followed by the most unexpected sound of all – laughter.

'Shaded you just a tad, *amigo*,' laughed Tunney, spinning a .45 on his trigger finger in a blurring blue arc. 'You're dead.'

'You're still lagging that little bit between the clear and the shoot,' countered a grinning Olan Quill. 'And that could mean you might get to blast a deputy, but a fast sheriff would still shade you.'

Their voices carried in the hushed night and the

honest citizens of the one-horse border town could only watch and wonder. The fake gunfight had all the trappings of the real thing and there wasn't a single onlooker who hadn't expected to see a man die before their eyes, maybe two. It was a shock to realize it had all been a game, hard to believe two grown men would think it amusing to stage something as chillingly convincing as that and call it fun.

But Mac Tunney and Olan Quill from the Pecos Herd, bedded nearby on the plains, were still chuckling at the way they had hoodwinked Sneak Creek. The black comedy just enacted had indeed been fun, if not totally so.

For each guntipper had played out his part in the episode just as fast as youthful reflex and skill would allow. This was one of their techniques of honing their great skills, competing against one another in staged showdowns designed to refine, polish and weed out faults in expectation of the real thing – fighting Kansans.

So, shocked Sneak Creek was luckier than it realized as the 'boys' refilled their guns and strolled off towards the livery without any real blood having been spilled.

The sound of drunken singing washed out over the batwings of the Sourdough saloon, where trailhands, cooks and wranglers were tying one on at the end of one of the longest and driest stretches of the trail drive since quitting the Pecos. The two fast guns liked saloons, dancing and gambling but stayed away from the bar. Liquor dulled the nerve-ends, could blur the eye, might shave that all-important split-second off a man's clear-and-fire. They resembled prize-fighters in strict training for the Big Event and it was possible that North Texas,

16

the Panhandle or indeed Kansas itself had seen nothing quite like them before. Which was why cattle king Harlen McCord paid each man double his trail boss's salary, and considered them worth every cent.

The pair rode the way they handled guns, with consummate ease. Sneak Creek was glad to see them go, and the feeling was mutual. To the guntippers, an untidy place in the trail like this burg was simply a place to get laid, sucker the hicks and move on.

Following a day's rest next day the major's herd would be moving on to a genuinely worthwhile destination around a week's drive north, a place named Chisum.

It was a dusty Kansas town sprawled on the north bank of Burnt River where it carved out its last big bend before commencing its long run down into the south-east; a booming border town where once the herders had been welcome, but not any longer.

This was the 'forbidden' Kansas town to which the major had been directly heading, ever since learning of the recent ban on the Texas herds passing through Chisum.

Nobody ever told the hero of Shiloh where he might or might not go, and his young killers looked upon him as a revered father.

'Bet he's waiting up for us to make sure we didn't go getting ourselves killed or something,' speculated Quill, watching the stars.

'He might be waiting up but he won't expect us to turn up dead,' Tunney replied. His heavy mouth quirked at the corners. 'For who could do it?'

'For sure none of the hard-luckers and has-beens

17

we've shifted out of our tracks since quitting the Pecos.' Tunney leaned his hands on his saddle horn and hunched supple shoulders. 'Matter of fact, the going's been that easy gunwise that at times a man has to wonder just why the major figured he might need gunpower like you and me, why he combed the Big Bend for us then agreed to pay us like kings. Ever ponder on that one?'

'Sure,' Quill replied in his deep, unhurried voice. 'But I do know one thing. The boss is a close man with a dollar and it's for sure he didn't shell out for you and me just on account he liked our style.' He nodded his large head. 'We'll earn our keep long afore we ship at Dodge, you can be certain of that.'

'Sure hope so.'

Young Mac Tunney sounded as sincere as a man could be. They were not looking for some kind of milk-run in Kansas this summer. Far from it. The Big Bend's best had signed on in full expectation of earning their high fees. Which, in their case, meant plying their crimson trade with the guns.

And having listened for years to the tales, some highly embellished, of Kansan arrogance and the hostility of Kansan shipping-towns towards everything emanating from south of the Cimarron and the Red, Mac Tunney and Olan Quill saw themselves as men with a mission.

Texas pride was at stake.

Texas honour.

They couldn't wait.

Soon the cloud-shadowed plain was murmuring to the sounds of weary breathing in the night, the stirring and sometimes the groaning with weariness, the slow rhythmic chomping of a vast collective cud.

The two were passing through the sleeping herd where lonesome nighthawks rode slowly to and fro, singing or playing the harmonica to keep bovine nerves nice and relaxed in order that the herd might not be overtaken by any insane impulse to jump up at the slightest sharp sound and go stampeding off half-way to hell in a dozen different directions, as longhorns were prone to do.

They were right about their employer; they could see the figure of McCord hunched before the chuckwagon fire well before they reached the circle of firelight and stepped down.

'About time too.' The cattle baron had lost an arm at Shiloh but this in no way detracted from the image he presented as a tough, hard-driving cattle king still capable of doing anything his men might do and in many cases doing it better. The former soldier was vain and feisty, but no fool. Any time danger threatened the herd, he was always ready to step aside and allow these two young guntippers to take charge. He saw no point in keeping guard dogs and barking himself. 'What kept you?'

'Women.' Tunney grinned, hunkering down to pour coffee into a pannikin. 'Ten girls for every man in Kansas, Mr McCord, and not a virgin over ten years old. Ain't that right, pard?'

'I thought it was closer to eight,' Quill responded, poker-faced.

It was doubtful if the older man even heard as he rose to his feet. 'There's been news since you left.'

They looked up sharply. They saw his expression was sober.

'From the North?' Quill hazarded.

'From Chisum, to be exact,' the cattle baron replied. 'It seems they have hired a city marshal of a similar breed to the kind which the Jayhawkers have used against us in Dodge and Wichita.' He paused to allow that to sink in, noting the young men's instant alertness and interest, like they could smell gunsmoke already. Then he added quietly, 'He's called the Gunner.'

'Jackman!' Tunney breathed. 'You wouldn't be kidding us, would you, boss?'

'I'm afraid it's only too true,' McCord said stiffly. 'Apparently their corrupt Town Board realized that Chisum might need some stiffening in the law department to help enforce their contemptible ban on visits by our trail crews, and elected to wheel in Marshal Jackman.'

'Wooee! They claim that bastard's the goddamn best!' Tunney said, impressed. He shot his partner a quick look. 'Or at least he used to be. . . .'

'Meaning?' snapped McCord. His knowledge of the world of gunmen or peacemakers was limited, but Tunney and Quill were encyclopaedic on the subject.

'They say he ain't the man he once was, boss,' supplied Quill. 'Leastwise that's what they said in that book on the Gunner that came out last—'

'He shot up and drove off a bunch of cowboys who jumped him on the train to Plainsville,' McCord cut in roughly, moustache bristling. 'Does that sound like the man's slipping?'

He waited for their reaction, half-expecting the pair to display apprehension. Instead they laughed delightedly and exchanged thumbs-up signals, acting as though they had just been dealt full hands.

The big man from the Pecos sighed windily and shook his head. He knew he would never understand this deadly new breed which seemed to have sprung up flourishing like poisonous weeds from out of the long Texas grass since the war. He did know, however, that he was now doubly pleased he'd shown the foresight to sign them on now that Jackman had entered the lists up North.

Ever since returning to his Pecos grass empire following last year's drive, Harlen McCord had made plans to deal with any serious trouble he might encounter upon his return to that border town this season. Not so much trouble with Kansas law, as with a certain Kansan power-broker by the name of Klegg Sands. What lay between the rich men from Chisum and the Pecos was deeply personal. The two had unfinished business, and the news on Clay Jackman convinced the cattleman that Sands was behind the town tamer's appointment, specifically aimed not at the expected Texas invasion of his town but at himself personally.

McCord prided himself on his foresight. Even he had realized that his wild waddies had run wild in the North last season, so he expected the Kansan towns to react this year. To counter whatever steps they might take, he'd outlaid serious money to hire a pair of his high-priced gunslingers as extra security, who now might be called upon to deal with a town-tamer known to every Texan cowman between the Red and the Rio Grande.

The Gunner might well be the ace in this big card-game they were now engaged in. But in Tunney and Quill the major believed he held both Left and Right Bower.

CHAPTER 2

THE MARSHAL'S WAY

'Something wrong with that dollar piece, Mr Marshal?'

Jackman gave no sign he had heard the saloonman's question. He was studying the change the Republic bartender had just pushed across the bar to him. There was nothing wrong with the coin, Jackman knew, yet its shape appeared almost elliptical, the edges fuzzed and not sharply defined.

He glanced away, blinked once, then checked the coin again. Now it appeared normal. Was his eyesight worsening further or was he slipping into the habit of looking for signs of advancing age where there was none. He slipped the coin into his pocket and picked up his whiskey glass.

'I sure don't understand why you won't allow a man to treat you a shot, Marshal Jackman,' complained big-bellied Brawn Carter, Sands's lieutenant, board member and one of those who paid their new peacemaker's generous salary. The man tried a smile. 'It against your religion or something?'

Jackman took a pull of his drink. Good whiskey. Strong but mellow. He took another taste. Carter appeared edgy. The man wasn't sure if the marshal was responding to him or not. He found the new lawman to be a totally different breed from their careworn sheriff. Sheriff Latigo could talk your leg off. In truth, if he could run a town as well as he could jaw there would be no need for Jackman.

'I never compromise my office, Mr Carter,' the marshal said gravely.

'Compromise . . . compromise?' The saloonman was having trouble getting across the word when a smooth voice sounded from behind.

'Marshal Jackman is quite correct, Brawn. A man in his position must not only be able to enforce the law but demonstrate that he is prepared to administer it impartially without taint of preference or prejudice. Is that not right, Marshal?'

Klegg Sands was a tall man, as tall as Jackman himself, an easy-smiling businessman of fifty summers. He was clean-shaven and wore an air of refinement as comfortably as another might wear a cloak. Class was reflected in the careful smile, the shrewdness of his gaze and the impeccable quality of his tailored suit. He nodded amiably.

'Nice to see you out and about, Marshal. I looked for you earlier today but didn't see you.'

'I keep my own hours.' Jackman's tone was sharp, almost brusque. He was naturally wary of any man who appeared too wealthy, sure of himself and much too

23

polite to be totally trusted. Nor was he overly taken with Brawn Carter, fatter, less successful, but possibly just as ambitious as the mayor. But such assessments and impressions had nothing to do with his remoteness of manner tonight.

He was simply weary.

This irked him. He viewed tiredness as a weakness, had no time for human frailty. Or for men who kept regular hours, for that matter. 'At times I sleep all day and work nights, or not at all. It all depends.'

'On what?' demanded blunt Carter.

'On the situation.' Jackman drained his glass and set it down on the bar as if its placement was of great importance. 'When it's quiet there is nothing to be gained burning the midnight oil. But when things are jumping, a lawman needs to be there around the clock if needs be.'

The board members traded looks and nodded as though in agreement.

'Er, touching on matters of importance, Marshal,' Sands went on in his ingratiating way, 'the sheriff came to me today with some story about your plans to shift the jailhouse into the courtroom and vice versa.'

'That's fact not gossip,' Jackman stated. 'The court-room is under-used and there will be more people going through the jail system from here on in. I intend conducting regular show-ups in the courthouse as I settle into my duties, and space will be required. From now on, the law office will conduct itself at a venue and in circumstances in which the people can come and see law being dispensed publicly in a way that will restore their confidence in the office. I've arranged for the work to begin tomorrow.'

Klegg Sands's urbane smile was proving hard to hold.

'I would have thought such an important decision might have better been made by you working in conjunction with the board, Marshal.'

'I will consult with the board when matters warrant, Mr Sands, not for every piddling day-to-day detail. Excuse me.'

The board men appeared to lean closer to one another across the mahogany as they watched the marshal's tall figure recede towards the doors.

'What do you think, Brawn?'

'Well he sure seems hard enough for the job. But he strikes me as uppity, and he ain't exactly an easy *hombre* to get along with, is he?'

'Not exactly.' Sands tapped his chin thoughtfully. 'Yet I suspect he shapes up overall as even more impressive than we dared hope. And that bloody business on the Dodge City train certainly demonstrated what he is capable of. I have the suspicion that Marshal Clay Jackman might be less easy to control than I'd hoped . . . yet the more I think about him the better suited he seems to be to fit in with my long term plans for him.'

'You mean your plans for the Pecos herd?'

Suddenly Klegg Sands wasn't looking smooth and genial any longer. His jaw set hard and his knuckles whitened as he clasped his glass tight.

'McCord,' he said thinly, then nodded. 'Uh-huh, that's what I'm talking about, mister. Won't be long before that mucker will be showing up, then our hard-jawed new law-bringer will find out he'll have to really

25

work for the big money the board is paying him.'

'If I had half a notion what you're talking about I might be a lot better off, Mr Sands.'

'You'll find out soon enough. Suffice it to say that McCord's horned in on my life once too often ... trying to beat my time with a certain lady, as well as trying to overrun my position here the way he did on last year's drive to the railhead.' He nodded emphatically. 'This is going to be war, and in war there can be but one winner. So, pour me a double and have one yourself, Brawn. The toast is to the marshal's success and a stemming of the Texan tide this season.'

Carter poured with one beefy hand, the other massaging the white scar on his thick neck, a memento of the last big riot involving Texans during the previous drive season. 'Hell, I'll drink to that any old day, Mr Mayor.'

On the street, Jackman paused to glance back at the Republic saloon, then allowed his gaze to rove over Mace Street, now beginning to throb with life again following the late afternoon lull.

His grey eyes were thoughtful and his ears missed nothing.

From further along Mace past River Street and The Deadline, which was the demarcation line between the semi-respectable element of Chisum and the anything-goes wild underbelly of the place, came the clear sound of four evenly spaced shots. Shooting like that rarely indicated trouble, he mused; they were too deliberate and methodical. Likely some clown from the herd bedded out on the plains was simply burning powder at the early stars for the hell of it, was his guess. But if he were wrong, and trouble it proved to be, he knew he would hear about it soon enough.

The main thing was that it was not cattlemen trouble. A herd had passed through three days prior to his arrival and nothing more was due for another couple of days. Time for Chisum's new badgeman to settle in some more, get the lie of the land and plan his strategies for dealing with the problem of the Texans, which for this border town appeared to be proving an exercise of dangerous dimensions.

The first sod of Chisum had been turned over but five years earlier by several enterprising entrepreneurs, including Klegg Sands who had quickly risen to the top of the heap.

The irony of the current situation was that the town's main reason for its very existence was the cattle trade. Situated far enough south of the railroad for it to hold attraction as a resting station for men and cattle before they made the final push for the shipping yards, it was an accommodating and entertaining kind of place which had quickly caught on to and fulfilled its original purpose, namely to attract the trail herds coming through and siphon off their excess dollars in return for goods and service at a price for which they could not be had further north.

So far so good.

But eventually old North-South antagonisms had reared their heads, leading to violence, riots, several killings and more than one lynching in recent seasons.

The herds kept coming but the attitude of the riders had changed. They now showed up angry and looking to get square for past offences, both real and imagined, said to have been committed against their fellow Lone Star Staters. A deputy was shot dead and a section of Rivertown put to the torch. There were incidents and reprisals, gunfights and back-alley stabbings. Until a meeting was called early on in the year's shipping season and Klegg Sands had led a surprising yet successful movement resulting in an official decision to shut the gates at a date to be fixed.

After the shut-down there were no more brawling, feuding or gun-happy Texas cowpokes roaming the streets of Chisum with bottles and guns in their hands and hate in their hearts.

Let them save that up and vent it upon the railroad towns further north, seemed to be the prevailing sentiment here. This town was off limits to anyone driving even just one single longhorn steer.

It proved a popular decision. But it was one thing to proclaim a law or ordinance and quite another to enforce it, as Jackman knew only too well.

Which was the reason that this starry night found him making his leisurely long-legged way along the main street, guns riding his hips and citizens giving way before his tall figure on the walks. The board had been forced to hire him to handle a job of work that sheriff and deputies plainly could not, but now he was here he received full support.

For Jackman, there was a satisfying familiarity about Chisum. It was just another in a long parade of two-gun frontier towns, living fast and hard, often dying just as suddenly as they were born. A few would survive, grow quieter and more respectable. In such places progress would eventually replace the wildness and eventually policemen on the beat would replace the sheriff and the two-gun town-tamer.

Would he last long enough to see that time come?

For a time he simply stood motionless, outwardly aloof and remote in brown suit and flat-brimmed hat as he briefly considered the uncertain future of a man skilled with the guns and experienced at handling the helltowns, but precious little else.

A specialist in a profession which might not last another ten years. Maybe not even five.

He brushed a hand over his jaw, moved on. Don't think too much, Marshal, it gets you nowhere. Just do your job. You're good at that. Do what must be done in Chisum and let tomorrow look out for itself. Show yourself, let them see what they are up against; don't just wear the badge but be the marshal.

His steps eventually led him to the Painted Lady saloon – a name that brought him up with a jolt.

Painted Lady? No, it had to just a coincidence. He squinted. He could not properly see the name of the proprietor beneath the name.

He looked left, looked right. Nobody close at the moment. Almost furtively he slid his eyeglasses from an inside pocket and quickly fitted them on. He looked again, stiffened as he read the name beneath the title sign.

It was several minutes that seemed so much longer before he eventually stirred from a strange inertia. Slowly his gaze played over the long, low-roofed building with its small illuminated windows and slow-smoking chimney-pots. Blazing brands set in barrels of earth illuminated the façade of the wild town's only saloon to be operated by a woman. It was a single-storeyed building with a curved false-front surmounted by a wooden painted cut-out of a female figure dancing, showing plenty of leg. It was situated almost on the Deadline, which meant it catered to both classes, the almost-respectables and the wild-and-woollies.

Nothing so remarkable about any of it, he supposed, but for that name carved into a piece of pine above the awning.

Carla Fallon; Prop.

Carla Fallon had run a smaller place up at Broken Bit where Jackman had spent one rainy fall and a bitter winter hammering law and order into the quartz-hard heads of a hundred hardrock miners with the barrels of his sixguns, taming Broken Bit with such ruthless efficiency that it eventually just shrivelled up and faded away from an excess of law and respectability.

Operation successful but the patient died.

He'd never expected to see Carla after they broke up in Broken Bit.

Eventually the new marshal of Chisum stirred to straighten his hat and flick something off his lapel as the fitful torchlight lifted his tall and sombre figure from the gloom.

And he wondered if this were vanity or some unbidden desire to impress? Or did he simply just want to make sure he conveyed exactly the same note of detached authority that had marked his tenure in other places, such as hell-raising Broken Bit, where he and Carla Fallon had once been so much more than friends.

He wanted to appear the same man he'd been

before that ominous day when the calendar turned and revealed that he'd turned forty . . . and the first seeds of self-doubt were sown. . . .

He straightened and shook his head. No. He couldn't allow Carla's presence here to affect his work in any way. He would not.

She, above all, must never suspect his self-doubt. Nobody should. And that went double for any man, North or South, who failed to respect the badge.

He moved forward, then halted as the figure appeared on the gallery above him.

The yellow lanternlight daubed his plaid shirt, and made the thick corded forearms, the familiar rugged face, glow like bronze.

His voice was without expression.

'Howdy, Bowie. Been a time.'

The powerful 'breed stood with boots wideplanted, nodding his big head. 'Indeed it has, sir.' Respectful but not deferential. Friendly enough yet reserved. Carla's Man Friday was nobody's man except his employer's. He had filled the roles of barkeep, bouncer and bodyguard for his mistress in Broken Bit, and Jackman was hardy surprised to find him with her here in Chisum. 'Come to visit with Miss Carla, have you Marshal Jackman?'

The nuances in the man's tone were not lost on him. Bowie was both welcoming and warning at the same time. Translated, the words might well mean: *Miss Carla will be pleased to see you, but you had better not mess up her life again.*

Jackman mounted the steps. He was taller but Bowie was wider. He packed twin Colts and a sneak derringer, but the 'breed, as always, was unarmed.

'How is she, Bowie?'

'Just fine.' The man gestured. 'Place doing well. Miss Carla is happy . . . and of course she has made plenty friends. . . .'

Again Jackman nodded. He knew what was meant. In Broken Bit, Carla's Nordic beauty had proved a magnet for males ranging from railroad tycoons sporting diamond stickpins to roaring Cro-Magnon Cousin Jacks from the mines who bathed but once yearly whether they felt they needed it or not.

He knew she would still be attractive to men at eighty; the 'breed didn't have to labour that point.

'By way of contrast, I don't expect to make any friends here,' he stated flatly. 'All I expect from people is that they obey the law. And that covers employing excessive violence in handling troublemakers in public places such as saloons. I trust I make myself clear?'

Bowie's face closed. Jackman had closed the man off. It was intentional. He played no favourites, less now than ever. The 'breed had warned him and he was warning him back. If it got to be a game in this town it was one he expected to win. He always did. The day a peacemaker lost was most often the same day they buried him.

'Whatever you say, Marshal sir. Miss Carla is inside.'

He was disturbed by the ache he felt when he sighted her standing by the piano talking to a bar girl. She was as lovely as ever, he saw at a glance. But there was something different about her and he soon realized what it was. Carla was not simply a girl fighting to make her way in a man's world any longer. She was a woman, and it was a woman poised and confident who came forward to extend both hands to him with a roomful of drinkers and gamblers who were watching with sharpened interest.

'Clay. How lovely to see you again.'

'Thanks, Carla. Same here.'

It was formal, yet did he detect an underlying warmth that he might not have expected following their break-up, seemingly an eternity ago?

But swift on the heels of that thought came another. He'd always proved most effective in towns where he was a total stranger. In such a situation, literally everyone was a potential enemy, and he treated them as such. But he and Carla went a long way back, which might prove a problem. Furthermore, she was now operating a sizeable saloon, and experience had taught that most of the troubles that erupted in frontier towns emanated from such establishments. He could only hope she ran an orderly place here. He would not care to come down on her if it proved otherwise, although knew he would if he must. When it came to law and order, the former marshal of Broken Bit, Jacknife and Buckhorn played the game strictly by the book.

They took a drink at the bar and it was almost like Broken Bit all over again; the tall marshal, the handsome saloon woman, the interested onlookers. But a river of time had passed by since Broken Bit, as the marshal was soon reminded.

'Are you unwell, Clay?'

'Never fitter.'

'If you say so.'

'You don't seem convinced, Carla.'

'It's not really my business to believe you or other-wise, is it?'

'Then . . . you don't think I look well, I take it?'

'You look . . . how might I put it? Tired? Yes, that's it. You never seemed tired before, as I recall.'

He nodded. She was as perceptive as ever. He was less relaxed or sure of himself now than when they had been together. He was annoyed that it showed. He glanced at the bar mirror and felt reassured. To his own eye, he didn't appear any different. He searched in vain for any hint of uncertainty or doubt, found none. The image that looked back at him looked just about the same as usual. Yet glancing sideways he still detected concern in dark eyes.

'Can't see it,' he said.

'You're thinner. Your face has grown gaunt. I'm not being critical, Clay, I'm just telling you the truth.' Her expression turned wry. 'But of course I can understand your surprise at my remarks. If you still operate the way you did back then, there would not be many people who would dare tell you the truth.'

There it was, he thought. The barb. Things had not changed all that much. The work and his dedication to it had been the rock upon which their romance had perished. He was, according to Carla Fallon, simply too much a twenty-four-hour-a-day badgeman to have time or interest left over for anything outside.

And, of course, she was right about his condition. He might be able to squint at his image in a looking-glass and convince himself that he looked pretty much the same Clay Jackman who'd trodden the dangerous turf of a dozen roaring helltowns. But if he were to set pride and vanity aside for a moment, and take an honest look, he suspected he might see exactly what the past two years had cost him. What had once been almost easy for him had slowly become hard. He worried on occasions now where he had never done so before. He suspected he'd been eroded by the years of danger and the bloodshed, and now he carried that secret with him every time he faced danger. That sort of knowledge did things to a man, even someone like him.

Yet he knew he could handle this job, and the one after that. He wouldn't be here if he thought otherwise.

Suddenly he smiled. 'Hey! Been talking to you five minutes and I haven't asked the most important question of all. How's Johnny?'

Her face softened, the way it always did at mention of her younger brother.

'He's fine, Clay. You won't believe how he's grown. He's been counting the days to your arrival. . . .' Her voice trailed away and she frowned.

'What is it, Carla?'

She shrugged and looked away. 'Do you know what they call him here? The boy sheriff.'

'I don't understand. Why would they—?'

She stared at him directly, almost accusingly. 'He's trying to be another you, Clay.' She spread her hands. 'Another town tamer and hero. He spends a lot of time at the law office and I've lost count of the times here that he's thrown drunks out or stopped brawls, things that should be left to the sheriff.' She shook her head. 'He still idolizes you.'

'I'm glad someone does,' he said with a small quirk of the lips.'Well,' he continued after a silence, 'I'd like to stop and talk some more, but I don't have to tell you what it's like for me in places like this, do I, Carla?' He forced a smile. 'It came as a surprise to find you in business here – a pleasant one, let me assure you.'

'I was thrilled when I heard you were coming.'

Thrilled? He was flattered and envious. Envious because he could not recall when he had last been 'thrilled' by anything.

'With luck we'll have a quiet time of it,' he said. 'I'm aware the Texas herders have been running riot, but often when they hear a town has signed on someone like me that proves enough to dampen them down and limit their mischief.'

She laughed.

'I know that. I've been warning my customers not to mess with the new marshal, and I think they are taking it to heart already.'

She suddenly sobered and turned her face away from him a little. 'Have you heard anything about Klegg Sands, Harlen McCord the cattleman, and myself, Clay?'

He frowned. 'How could I? I didn't even know that—'

'The simple story is that I appear to have attracted both men and this has created bad blood between them. Some people go so far as to suggest this could cause serious trouble when Harlen brings his Pecos herd this way again soon. I thought you should know about it.'

He nodded. 'Thanks for being candid, Carla.'

Now she met his gaze levelly. 'They are both twice my age, Clay. I expect I decided after our break-up, that in future I would go for wealth and security rather than. . . .'

Her words trailed off. Yet he nodded understandingly. He appreciated her candour. He certainly had no claim on her. And Carla would attract suitors if stranded in Death Valley in midsummer.

He was framing a response when it happened.

'All right,' the voice bellowed from the street. 'Where is this wonderman of a Yankee-lovin' marshal I hear so much about. Iffen you are inside, better come out and meet Chot Valder, Mr Marshal, suh, otherwise I might have to sashay in and drag you out by your dick.'

The saloon fell silent. Jackman fitted his hat to his head and ventured a small smile.

'Some things never change, do they, Carla?'

She placed a hand on his arm.

'Why am I afraid for you as I never was before, Clay? Why is that?'

'Jackman, you dog-eatin' whoremaster! Show your Union blue ass out here. I ain't a patient man.'

Now he welcomed the interruption; it was his excuse to escape that searching look in her eyes.

'You and I are not the afraid breed, Carla,' he said. 'Remember?'

Then tipping his hat he went out through the batwings to face the trouble-hunting Texan.

CHAPTER 3

HIT THEM HARD

Chot Valder never knew what hit him. One moment he was standing in the street, handing the approaching lawman a Brazos River mouthful of drunken curses, the next something exploded against the side of his skull like a grenade and he knew no more until coming to in the cells with the granddaddy of all headaches and what seemed like a yard of bed sheeting wrapped around his sorry head.

'He'll be fine, Marshal,' the little man with the black medical bag assured the tall figure seated behind the lamplit desk up front. 'Mild concussion and a reasonably deep ear lesion which required some stitching. Nothing new for this character, judging by the scars he displays.'

Doc Walsh turned to the burly figure of the sheriff seated in the cane chair below the gunrack.

'Bit different from last week when he attacked you, eh, Sheriff?'

The lawman nodded lugubriously. Some days earlier,

38

following the marshal's official appointment by the town board, Chot Valder from the Brazos had jumped the sheriff in a dark alley and knocked two of his teeth out, then taken a chancy shot at a deputy who came to his assistance. The Texan had evaded arrest on that occasion, which had given him the courage and ambition to seek to climb a notch higher by taking on the new man behind the badge tonight.

'He'll think twice before kicking up his heels again, I reckon,' the doctor predicted, throwing an admiring glance at Jackman.

Tonight was the marshal's first real taste of action, although he had already featured in several arrests and confrontations during his short time behind the badge. Valder was widely regarded as a dangerous man and a formidable brawler. His defeat at the marshal's hands must send alarm signals running through the ranks of the lawless, or the sheriff was no judge. 'It's something I'd like to have seen, Marshal. How'd you do it?'

Jackman shrugged.

'He was drunk, over-confident and it was half-dark, Sheriff. He didn't have much of a chance actually.' Then he glanced at the medico. 'That ear will heal?'

'Sure. Cut like that's more like a lover's caress to a rock-headed Texican, Marshal. Even so, you must have really laid your gunbarrel in to cut that deep.'

Jackman made no reply.

Whenever there was no other option but to go after a man, he always went in hard. With this rough-headed waddy it had been no different. He had been able to come clear with his piece and bring it against the side of the skull before the fellow even knew he was in danger. Yet the marshal's satisfaction was muted by the awareness that he had aimed his cut with the gunbarrel above the ear. Nothing to fret about really, he mused. Could simply mean his timing was a little off due to a longer than usual lay-off between assignments.

He squinted and rubbed at his eyes. The doctor leaned forward with lamplight splashing upwards over his little gnome's face.

'Are you sure you're all right, Marshal Jackman?'

'Of course I'm all damned right. Why shouldn't I be? On your way, Doctor, I've work to do. And it might be an idea to get in a good night's rest as I intend paying a visit to the Cowboy's Rest tomorrow as I'm of the opinion that some of those gentlemen from south of the border have overstayed their welcome. Could be your services will be required again if I meet unlawful opposition.'

He was back on the street within minutes.The mood of the town had changed. He sensed it immediately. Knots of Texan drovers stood talking on street corners, falling silent at his approach, starting up again only when he had passed.

Texas vanity had been wounded. The solid thud of a sixgun barrel contacting a hard Texan skull made a sound that carried from one end of this trail town to the other.

Ever since the driving season began and Chisum was yet again the stopover destination for many of the herds coming up through Lubbock, Amarillo, Wichita Falls and Elk City, tired riders, fired riders and riders returning from the railroad in the north with pay-checks in their Levis had been swelling the population and making life difficult in Chisum.

Late last season, a rioting Texas mob had been responsible for the death of the then sheriff; his replacement had taken over in midwinter. This was hailed as a Texas triumph and the mood of those herders in town now was still buoyed up as a result of that 'victory'. Jackman's shock appointment had only succeeded in temporarily putting a dampener on Texan excess and belligerence, it had not eliminated it.

But now that a relatively senior member of the booze-and-brawl faction had been dealt with and with such scant respect, there was an uneasy air of tension and uncertainty as the wild men took a second look at the Kansan town-tamer before pondering their next play.

Jackman hoped it would prove to be a major play when it came, as he knew it must. Experience had taught him that the quicker you moved in and asserted your authority the more positive and dramatic the effect. It was the towns that simmered and burbled indefinitely that most tended to erupt eventually when least expected, and the town-tamer was determined to do what he could to avoid such a situation evolving here.

Nine times out of ten, sooner proved better than later.

The large group assembled on the long front porch of the Lone Star saloon comprised nothing but Texans. This pridefully named watering-hole was their club, meeting-house and bastion of Texas hostility and jingoism. 'Kansan' was almost a pejorative expression at the Lone Star. It had yet to be visited by the board's new appointment; this situation was about to be rectified.

Without pausing, Jackman swung in off the street and started straight up the steps. A man standing there deliberately moved to block his path. Out came the sixshooter and next instant the waddy was rolling down the steps with blood streaming from his forehead.

'Yes?' Jackman challenged, shoving a gun muzzle into the lean gut of a beanpole saddlebum who was making uncertain clawing movements at his own gun. 'Go ahead, boy. Take it out and they can bury you by moonlight tonight before I clear the lot of you out at daybreak. Well, what are you waiting for, saddlebum?'

A score of Texans gaped in awe, stunned and off-balanced. The marshal didn't afford them time to recover. Contemptuously he turned his back on the would-be gun-thrower, yet made certain that everyone saw him holster his piece and deliberately draw the skirts of his coat over both thornwood grips before continuing.

'I've been examining the records concerning visitors to this town and find little to convince me that you gentlemen are not a bunch of stinking lawbreakers taking advantage of the drives to act in a way you would never be permitted to do back home in Brushpopper or Latrine On The Brazos. This liberty will be no longer permitted and you are all hereby officially warned that I live by the book. If an offence is on the statute books here, then it will be strictly enforced, and you can believe it shall be enforced forcefully. Now, clear this street!'

Some moved but others stayed put.

The runt with curly hair and bowed legs was one of the latter.

'We ain't done nothin' that you can move us off the street for, Jackman. That ain't on the books nowhere. This is all USA. It ain't Mexico or Africa or somethin'. We know our rights.'

'So, it was right to murder a lawman here then?' Jackman snapped.

'We wasn't even here when that happened,' chimed in another. 'You got no right to—'

Jackman's coat panel flapped, a Thuer Colt conversion model .45 magically appeared in his right hand and a score of startled cowpunchers ducked low as the roar of the shot slammed against their ears and filled the porch with billowing white smoke.

'Don't you talk rights to me, mister!' Jackman snapped. 'Not after the murder of a peace officer and enough misdemeanours, crimes and offences to fill a volume, you won't. Understand this. Your rights here are as I identify them. And if my interpretation of the rules and regulations here are not on the books yet, they very soon will be. Now I surely dislike giving an order twice.' He lowered the still smoking Colt. 'I'm waiting to see you obey it.'

In less than a half-minute he had the porch all to himself, with big-hatted figures receding along the street while a second bunch assembled on the gallery of the Clayton House opposite to stare.

Jackman put the gun away.

His actions had been authoritarian and he would be first to admit it. But this had been deliberate, for he considered the ends justified the means. He had chosen the moment to introduce himself to the perceived foe in the only way they understood. Now they would either absorb the lesson and take it to heart, or else they would get together, prime themselves up on liquor and outraged pride and come looking for him.

He would not be hard to find.

When young Johnny Fallon quit the barroom on River Street there was an eagerness in his step. He'd been out of town when Clay showed up, hadn't even known he had arrived until he returned to Chisum that night only to find he'd missed all the action, first at Sis's place then at the Lone Star. He felt he'd been cheated some-how, and was in no frame of mind to accept anything untoward from anyone wearing a four-gallon hat or boasting a Texas accent.

A man brushed past him as he passed the barber-shop, and Fallon whirled and glared. The man paused, saw who it was, muttered: 'Damn fool kid,' and contin-ued on his way, a burly figure in a billowing slicker.

'Would you care to come back and repeat that, Ryan?' Johnny called after him.

The cowboy paused and half-turned. He'd not been in town long and hadn't had time to figure out tall Johnny Fallon. Some saddle partners insisted the young man was a joke, a part-time worker at his sister's saloon and apparently some kind of honorary peace officer. Others chose to give him a wide berth on account of stories – rumours mainly – that 'the kid' was far tougher and more competent than he looked.

After a bit the waddy shrugged and kept walking. 'And keep away from the saloon and my sister, saddle stiff!' Fallon called after him. He sometimes adopted the high moral ground as his sister's champion and protector, this despite the fact that Carla was probably more than capable of looking after herself, and had ably demonstrated this quality since their parents passed away, leaving her with a living to make and a then teenage brother to look out for.

His sister didn't seem to realize that Johnny was now a full grown man with broad shoulders and a growing reputation as an unofficial deputy with friends at the jailhouse, and a deepening civic concern for Chisum and its citizens.

Tall and light-footed, the young man strode on, keeping a sharp eye peeled for his 'pal' Clay, and scowling whenever he sighted a Texan. Despite his youth, Johnny Fallon was an outspoken member of the increasing anti-Texan faction headed by Klegg Sands, which was drawing more support from the community as the current trail season gathered momentum.

The fact that the young man frequently clashed with the aliens from Texas notwithstanding, he was still generally regarded as mainly a minor irritant by most long riders from the south.

Some were of the view that Johnny's involvement with the law might have by this landed him in far more serious trouble with the Texans than it had done, considering that few herders wanted to risk getting on to the wrong side of the lovely Carla by tangling with the kid brother. Besides, most Texans liked to regard themselves as big men dealing with important issues and enemies on the Kansas side of the border, such as lawmen and troopers, or big-bucks sons of bitches like Klegg Sands, who'd grown fat on the Texas trade and now wanted to pull the plug on it. There were bigger fish to fry here than Johnny Fallon for a proud and North-hating rider from the Panhandle, or so many chose to believe. Johnny's view was that there was a critical shortage of strong men in his new home town, and as a consequence could scarcely believe his good fortune when he heard that the board had hired Clay Jackman as city marshal, that in fact the man he admired most was actually here in Chisum patrolling its streets right now.

The very last time he'd glimpsed Jackman in action he'd been down on one knee under a blazing sun in Deacon Street, Broken Bit, Colt in either hand and hat lying in the dust with a hole through the crown, shooting it out with the Burkes.

The Burkes were migrant Ozark hill men with a burning grudge against miners, outsiders and all authority whatever shape it might assume.

With Broken Bit booming on the back of a big strike at that time, Johnny would never forget what it had been like to witness Jackman's courage and ability at first hand.

That day he'd seen wild men go down in the dust as big leaden hammers smashed into them, breaking them apart inside and imposing the iron will of the law in the final, fatal way.

In the end four wild men lay dead and the only visible injury to Jackman, as he got to his feet, was just that single bullet hole in the crown of his hat.

That was a scene etched in Johnny Fallon's memory to this day. He had witnessed other similar scenes involving Jackman before the marshal resigned and moved on. But that was the one that stayed in his mind

46

and was the reason Jackman had become an icon in his imagination.

The fact that Jackman and Carla eventually became lovers, and the marshal the growing boy's companion and protector, was more than sufficient to make the badgeman's last few months in the Bit the happiest of Johnny Fallon's life.

Whether because of his relationship with Carla, or for some entirely dissociated reason, Jackman eventually took him under his wing and became his hero and best friend as a result.

Small wonder he was hurrying through the night streets looking for the marshal right now, sore that he'd missed out on so much excitement already yet tingling with the anticipation of just how much things were destined to change when Chisum realized exactly who it was now wearing the marshal's star.

His steps led him eventually to the smithy where his friend Augie Gee worked as a striker. Augie had followed Johnny and his sister from the West. The two had been buddies since boyhood. Some thought Augie a little simple, but not Johnny Fallon. He and Augie had always gotten along just fine, and apart from that, he trusted the husky youngster.

He found his friend taking a breather and a smoke out back of the ramshackle smithy where he spent his days slamming hot metal into shape by a roaring forge. They greeted in the usual exuberant way, throwing fake punches, ducking and weaving and trading insults. Johnny loved this sort of interchange when he could act just like a kid, for it was said, and may have been true, that he could be too serious-minded for a boy of his age.

The two were seated on a crate in the sunlight talking about girls and the new marshal when a Texan ducked into the yard from the back alley and began unbuttoning his fly.

'Hey!' Johnny called. 'Go next door where—'

'Don't tell me what to do, kid, 'the man growled.

'You're breaking the law,' Johnny snapped, heading towards him.

'Go tell the crummy marshal, why don't you?'

Johnny's jaws muscles worked. 'Do up those buttons and drag your sorry ass out of this yard or I'll—'

The man cursed and charged. He was red-faced from hard liquor and had lost money at cards that morning. He wasn't taking jaw from anybody's kid brother, and threw a punch meant to prove it.

Johnny danced out of range, then came back in close and hooked to the jaw. The cowboy stopped on a dime, eyes beginning to glass over. 'The law, bonehead!' Johnny shouted, then knocked him on the seat of his britches with a short straight left that a prizefighter might have been proud of.

The Texan was still sprawled motionless in the grass when Brawn Carter and two sidekicks from the Republic showed up. To the astonishment of the bystanders looking over the side fence, the men moved right in, acting like Fallon's friends, which they surely never had been.

'Bring that bum round and warn him not to mess with any pal of mine, boys,' Carter instructed officiously. Then he gave Johnny a big grin. 'There's more important things for you to be doin' than brawling with cowhands, boyo.'

Johnny stepped back, suspicious but curious. He disliked this man and had no reason to trust him or anything he said. Yet of late he was disciplining himself to be less rigid and critical in his adopted town.

Plainly Carter's arrival on this scene was not entirely accidental. The greedy eyes and fat mouth warned him the man wanted something. But what?

He decided to find out.

He put on a grin and Carter threw an arm about his shoulders, adopted a confidential manner now.

'Kid . . . kid, you're wasting your time in this man's town, playing amateur sheriff, cosying up to losers like Sheriff Latigo and ruckusing with likkered-up trail herders like that bum. What if I was to tell you that the biggest man in town's had his eye on you for quite a spell, and that there's nothing he'd like more than to set down and have a long quiet yarn about you and him and the future? And I'm talking a real future here. Big bucks, big opportunities, big times. Wanna hear any more?'

'Who are we talking about, Carter?' He was trying not to act suspicious, but how could he help it?

Carter paused for effect. 'No less a man than Klegg Sands, is who.'

Johnny felt himself stiffen. He carried a list in his head of those men who might be conspiring to Chisum's detriment and their own advantage, and Sands was up near the top of that list. And the man was chairman of the board.

The boy in him still wanted to tell Brawn Carter to move on, but it was the man he was rapidly becoming who framed the wary answer to the man's question.

49

'Why would Sands want to see me?'

The beefy face lighted up like a beacon. 'Why don't you let him tell you himself, kid?'

The blacksmith called Augie from the back window. The boy flicked a gesture at Johnny and slouched off. Johnny was barely aware of the boy's leaving. He rubbed his jaw, studying Carter's cunning, punched-in mug. He was intrigued by but wary of the fellow's proposition. Carter grinned unconvincingly. Johnny had a debate with his cautious side, and his curiosity won out.

'All right,' he grunted. 'Let's go see what the man wants.'

'Spoken like a true winner, kid.' Brawn Carter chuckled, and within ten minutes Johnny Fallon found himself being ushered into one of the Republic's plush private rooms where Klegg Sands sat in a fat velvet chair smoking a Cuban cigar and smiling.

That smile made Roy edgy, for although suave, polished and unfailingly charming to pretty ladies, the city's Mr Big had a reputation and was known to be anything but a glad-hander or even easy to get along with behind his flashy, long-haired façade.

Sands had helped build Cimarron City from the ground up with the intention of growing fat on the trail-drive dollar, had done this with several associates but for a long time now his had been the sole hand on the tiller.

The president of the board and owner of a quarter of the town's real estate and developments mostly acted as though Carla Fallon's brother did not exist except when he sought to impress her, then he went overboard trying to be belatedly pleasant to the youngster.

'You wanted to see me, Mr Sands?'

'Sit down, sit down, Johnny.' An expansive gesture. 'Cigarette? Cigar?' Another smile. 'Oh, that's right. You don't smoke. Remember your sister telling me that. And by the way, how is Carla?'

'She's fine.'

'Splendid woman, your sister. Strong, independent. Loaded with class. . . .'

Johnny just nodded. He might be offended by Sands's obvious interest in his sister, but he knew that Carla was more than capable of looking out for herself.

He wondered if the big man might ask him to put in a good word for him with his sister. He'd never do that. Carla made her own decisions about men and nothing could influence her. From Johnny's point of view, the last smart decision she had made in the romantic sense was to fall for Clay Jackman in Broken Bit, even if there'd been a river of tears when the break-up came. But whoever said true love ran smooth?

Seated opposite the mayor across a rosewood table, Johnny quickly saw Sands's bogus goodwill fading fast.

In truth, Sands was actually in a foul temper bordering on the violent tonight. But it was not directed at Johnny. The man had questions about the new marshal he wanted answered, reckoned young Fallon was just the man who might be able to answer them.

'Clay?' Johnny asked warily. 'What about him?'

'A straight answer, Johnny. Is there still something between Jackman and your sister?'

Johnny was almost relieved.

So that was it!

He felt himself frown a moment later. He believed Sands was serious concerning his sister. He knew Sis led the big man on, for some reason – just the way she'd done the Pecos cattle king, McCord, last season. Whatever the truth, it was no business of his. But he was intuitive, sensed Sands was leading up to something.

'What gives you that notion about Sis and the marshal?' he heard himself ask.

'Jackman stopped by at the Lady today, so I'm told. They talked for quite a time, and afterwards a percenter saw your sister crying in a back room.'

Sands leaned forward, more intent and commanding than Johnny had ever seen him. Mr Big claimed to be in love with his sister. Maybe he was telling the truth for once.

'I questioned your damned 'breed doorman, but he was evasive. Too evasive by far. Then I asked your sister direct and she told me it was none of my damned business. But it is my business, boy. I must confess I mean to marry Carla someday soon and smother her, and you, in luxury. My intentions are honourable and I don't think it's too much for a suitor to know something that could prove of major importance regarding his sweetheart, do you, son?'

But the rich man would get nothing more out of Johnny Fallon now. The young man offered a few glib answers and soon found an excuse to get up and leave. He couldn't see Sis taking Sands seriously even before Clay showed; now he calculated Sands's chances as zero.

The door hissed shut on Johnny's back and a silence fell. Brawn Carter picked his teeth with a combination toothpick and ear-cleaner and studied his boss as the silence dragged on.

Although successful in his own right, Carter was still very much Sands's sidekick in major matters. The mayor virtually ran this town from the ground up as befitted the man who bossed almost everything from the water cartage concession up to who appointed judges or hired professional peace officers when the wheels of law seemed incapable of doing so.

Carter's privileged position brought the man many benefits. It also afforded him an insight into Sands's real character. As a confidant he happened to know the big man was genuinely obsessed by the ice-queen princess of the Painted Lady, so much so that he believed Sands was prepared deliberately to turn off the golden tap that was the Texan trade if this was what it took to make the woman Mrs Klegg Sands.

He knew Sands was hurting right now. For the irony here was that it had been Sands's decision that saw the board approve Jackman's response to their advertising for a professional capable of saving Chisum. The realization that in so doing he had imported a plainly difficult man to handle, along with potential or actual rival for the woman he lusted after, must have Sands eating his liver right now, as he finished off Johnny's barely touched drink.

But Sands could take hard knocks, didn't know what it was like to quit once having set his sights on a given target. There was a larger agenda here, something which in truth had been the real reason why Klegg Sands had authorized and largely financed the appointment of Clay Jackman in the first place.

Certainly he wanted the Texans reined in, banished if that was what was required. But it was not Texans in general who preoccupied him at this tense moment, but rather a Texan, namely Major Harlen McCord from the Pecos whose herd was, at that very moment, camped somewhere out on the Panhandle plains with its longhorn muzzles pointed directly towards Chisum.

McCord must be dealt with first for reasons only Sands and Carter understood.

The mayor hadn't known of the former relationship between Carla Fallon and the new marshal until after Jackman had arrived in town and taken up his post, by which time it was too late even for Chisum's Mr Big to do anything about that appointment.

Sands had planned all along to utilize Jackman in his attempt to rid himself of the Pecos herd boss and keep him away from Chisum and Carla.

It was commonly believed that the powerful Pecos cattleman had journeyed all the long miles from the Pecos to the railheads for the second time in succeeding years, partly in order to market his beef for top dollar, but primarily to resume his courtship of the city's most desirable woman!

Sands felt quietly in full command again when he and Carter set out for the jailhouse, where they waited an hour for the marshal to complete his duties processing offenders in the courthouse's show-up room, before getting to see him.

Jackman was duly informed that it was the wish of the board that their new marshal ride out and locate the Pecos herd next day and inform the Pecos herd that, for reasons he explained, the crew would not be granted permission to stop over at Chisum, not even briefly.

After considering this directive, Jackman soberly suggested that Major Harlen McCord might well find them extreme and possibly unacceptable.

'I agree, Marshal,' Sands replied unblinkingly. 'But if that proves to be the case then it's your duty to handle the situation, is it not?'

Jackman's response was immediate. 'Indeed it is,' he stated firmly. And didn't begin knuckling his eyes until the two were gone.

CHAPTER 4

WHEN FAST MEN FACE

She stood by her window with folded arms watching the two men she loved most with an expression of unease, tenderness and something bordering on envy.

After three long years Johnny and Clay were acting as if they'd never been apart, joking, talking incessantly, catching up. She'd even seen them sparring with one another as they'd done in Broken Bit, seemingly an eternity ago.

Men!

They were not simply a different sex but often could seem like a totally alien species! Didn't either of them realize she simply didn't want them taking up where they'd left off – Clay the hero town-tamer and Johnny his admiring understudy.

Everything was wrong about that scenario, in her eyes. She had armoured herself against the heartbreak involved in their break-up, and didn't welcome any situation that might bring them into one another's company more than might be necessary.

She was also considering the suit of a very rich, very powerful cattle king from the South, and she certainly didn't want Clay's presence complicating that.

But most of all she resented and felt betrayed by her own reaction to seeing Jackman again after three years. She had never expected it to be easy, but it was proving difficult, almost painful. So many memories.

Watching his tall figure now as the two sauntered about the stables and workshop in back of the saloon, she could still see how he'd aged, and yet that fluent graceful walk was unchanged, the grey at his temples giving him an air of distinction.

Johnny flipped him a battered old ball – just the way he did when horsing around with Augie. Clay caught it comfortably, yet, she was sure, not as surely as he might have once done.

They were all of them three years older, she reminded herself. She didn't drive her pony and gig as fast as she'd done back in Broken Bit, and Clay's eyesight was not as keen. The distinction was that driving more slowly didn't present any danger for her. Her life didn't depend upon her sureness and quickness of eye as his did. . . .

A flustered maid entered the room. 'Miz Carla, they're wrangling at the poker layout again.'

'So?'

'Well, you know what they're like, Miz Carla. If they get to ruckusin' they might just wreck the place.'

'Tell them I'll shoot anyone who breaks anything.'

'You really want me to tell them that?'

'I want you to disappear, Lizzie, that's what I want.'

'Yes'm.'

She turned back to the window to find two tall men standing directly below and smiling up at her. She saw that Johnny was twirling one of Clay's black revolvers on his finger. The young man flipped the weapon to Jackman who caught it and dropped it into the holster with effortless dexterity.

It was impossible not to be aware of the impression that action made on her brother.

Clay palmed the gun so fast even she could scarce believe it. Then he twirled the weapon on his trigger finger in a steel blur, tossed it overhead, caught it behind his back, grinning all the while.

She could barely recall ever seeing Clay acting frivolously. She shouldn't begrudge him that, this grim business he was in.

Carla leaned both hands upon the railing and turned to gaze south. Somewhere out there rode the Texan who insisted he was in love with her and wanted them to marry. Harlen McCord was impressive, intelligent and caring despite a wide reputation for North-hating ruthlessness. She wanted to believe he was the breed of man a woman might learn to love and even lean upon.

She wasn't aware that sometime soon, Clay Jackman would be saddling up and riding out to meet Harlen McCord bearing a long list of restrictions and an official document concerning the herd's proposed stopover which no proud Texas cattle baron could possibly accept.

*

The marshal mostly slept late. He could easily afford the best hotel room in town but instead was lodged in Room 22 at the Clayton House off Mace Street. The accommodation here suited his needs just fine. His was the last room in the upstairs corridor with a door giving on to the fire escape close by. Such an amenity had its advantages for any man who slept with one eye open and his hand wrapped round a gun butt. It meant that if he heard steps outside his door it was either the maid, the place was on fire, or there was some lowlife out there coming after him with a gun.

The maid had already been in to waken him. She was pert and pretty and seemed excited to have him staying with them. She imagined his work to be dashing, even glamorous. He had news for her.

His vision was at its clearest first thing in the morning and he donned his spectacles to study his surroundings comfortably as he rose and began to dress.

The room was twelve by ten, like all the others. The furnishings comprised bed, washstand, bureau and two sturdy plain chairs. There were extra hooks on the door for clothing that wouldn't fit into the bureau, and he had three suits hanging there.

The faded pink roses of the wallpaper were a reminder of middling to bad hotel rooms he'd occupied in other places. Occasionally he struck a luxury hotel where the security requirements met his special needs. He always took them when this applied, yet in truth the amenities, or lack of them, made little impression on Clay Jackman. Rooms were just someplace to sleep, punctuating the lengthy periods of time spent elsewhere presenting himself as a walking target for the hellers.

He poured water from the pitcher and shaved. Gaunt-looking, she had said. Maybe she was right. He certainly looked that way compared to the sleek smoothness of a Klegg Sands or the beefiness of Brawn Carter.

He frowned as the razor slid down one flat cheek.

Plainly there were wheels within wheels in Chisum, as was the case in every place he'd worked. Sure, the city fathers wanted the riot act read to the Pecos bunch, and the records on Texan troubles affirmed that this was a proper and sensible step to take. But he would still like to know what else had been disturbing Sands when they met last night. He reckoned he'd sensed an underlying resentment bordering on hostility in the board boss. Either that or he was getting to mistrust everyone more and more as time went by.

He finished shaving and dabbed the soap from his face before going to work on the guns with oil and rag.

It was an old, familiar chore which he followed slavishly every day, like a priest going through the sacred ritual of the Mass. The priest was intent on saving immortal souls and he was equally focused on preserving his very mortal life.

He'd seen men die because a gun misfired. He'd also seen them die because they apparently didn't see straight, but that was not something you could guard against with gun oil and a strip of calico.

The Thuer's conversion Colts were old but reliable. Their vital aspect to a man of his calling was that the ejection of spent shells was a simpler, faster operation than with the more modern Peacemaker. To eject the shells the recoil plate was revolved opposite the hammer, and the hammer snapped six times, ejecting the spent cartridges from the front of the revolving cylinder. Reloading, in reverse order, was equally quick and proficient.

A reliable tool, so well-suited to his deadly trade, the town-tamer thought sombrely. The few fractions of seconds saved in ejecting and reloading could save his life at the cost of another's; had done, and might well do so again.

Maybe today.

The sheriff had briefed him on the major from the Pecos and in so doing had unwittingly apprised Jackman of the cattleman's interest in Carla Fallon last season. Jackman already suspected Sands could well be carrying some kind of torch for her, but was not about to allow this factor to influence in any way his execution of the duty he had been assigned today.

Men like Sands, he was convinced, rarely allowed personal matters to divert them from the holy grail of their grasping lives, namely the acquisition of money, power and all the trappings. He believed profit and loss were behind Mr Big's directives, not something as intangible or unpredictable as love.

Standing at the window shrugging into his riding-jacket, he wondered what it would be like to have your goals all clear-cut and identifiable, in comparison to the ideals or demons which drove him.

At age forty-one he still did not know whether he was a bona fide career lawman who had acquired the gun skills to make his success possible, or simply a natural guntip-per – a 'gunner' as they named him – who had drifted into the law as a natural flow-on from such abilities.

And he ended up with the same old unanswerable question. Either way, did it really matter a damn?

Too much thinking for this time of day, he decided, and concentrated instead on knotting his black string-tie the way he liked it.

He took his leisurely breakfast-cum-early-lunch at the diner next door, then found his rented horse saddled and ready as ordered at the livery up on the next block.

He saw Carla waiting there, shaded by a flowered parasol, the moment he came within sight of the building.

For a moment he felt a hit in the heart. Thinking: was it going to be like old times again? Her waiting for him unexpectedly? The old easy rapport?

But he realized she was in sober mood as they met and exchanged greetings. And, Carla-like, she came right to the point.

She indicated the leather satchel he toted and asked directly whether it contained a posting order, designed to keep the Pecos herd out of town.

He shrugged. 'It's supposed to be confidential, Carla, but yeah, that's what it is.'

'Are they crazy? Harlen won't stand for this. Nor should he. Anyway, I'm sure it's illegal. In America, nobody can deny anybody access to any town. What. . . ?'

'Carla, I just follow orders, not make them up.'

'You realize what this is, of course, don't you? It's Sands trying to get rid of Harlen because he is jealous. It has nothing to do with the herders raising hell.'

He found himself studying her intently. Maybe this was a genuine civic concern she was expressing – and

62

quite possibly she could be right about the motivation behind the posting order. Yet he found himself wanting it to be something different. Like, finding an excuse to see him again.

'Maybe you're wrong,' he heard himself say. 'I hear the Pecos bunch really kicked over the traces here last time. Maybe Sands is wise to post them out of town?'

'I'll give Klegg a piece of my mind when I see him. In the meantime, Clay, you—'

'Will have to do as I'm ordered, Carla.'

'Well, I can see I'm wasting my time.' She sniffed and was gone, silk dress hugging her stunning figure, golden hair bobbing.

He shrugged and went inside to find his dapple-grey saddled and ready for the trail.

A surprising number of people were on the street as he rode down Mace Street making for the south trail. Looked like the word had got out that the Gunner would be riding out to meet up with the Pecos herd down south. Men and women who stood watching as the tall figure on the dappled grey trotted by were reassured by the formidable sight he presented, yet many remained plainly apprehensive. McCord's was a big outfit, and there was talk that the cattleman had brought along some extra guns to help counter the kind of opposition in the north that he and other cattlemen had encountered last summer.

Jackman had been warned about the same thing by the sheriff. Rightly or wrongly, it meant little to him, warranted no major change of plans. At times like this he relied on instinct to tell him when to push hard, back off, or fall back on the guns.

Too often in this trade, which men like Hickok, Masterson and the Earps had followed before him, the final resolution proved to be gunsmoke and blood. He accepted this. He was a practitioner, not an improviser. Over the years he had schooled most of the weaknesses to which men of his calling were vulnerable to from his system, until he had become almost the perfect law-enforcement killing machine.

And only he could know that he did not always clearly see what he shot at these days.

Dust stained the horizon. A big herd was on the move out there. Soon he sighted the chuckwagon jouncing towards him across the plain far ahead of the mob. The drovers behind would keep the mob rolling north until the cook located a suitable bedground, where he would be waiting for them at dusk, hot supper at the ready, and if they were lucky, their bedrolls spread out for them.

Marshal Jackman would be waiting with him.

He spent the late afternoon relaxing in a draw within sight of the spot where the cook had set up camp. As he sat with his cigars and his thoughts, the dust and the low rumbling of countless hoofs warned that him the Pecos herd was now approaching the bedground.

He resaddled the dapple-grey and yet again checked out his guns.

A mile distant a handsome coach and matched bays were wheeling in alongside the chuckwagon as travel-stained riders brought the huge herd to its camp-ground.

There was a small creek and it was the job of the drag riders to police the thirsty stock at their drinking to

64

ensure there was no milling or fighting, while the men who had spent the past fourteen hours keeping the 2000 head pointed in the right direction hurriedly washed up, grabbed their eating utensils and lined up for chow.

The marshal of Chisum was camped so close that he was within gun range of the camp before he was eventually spotted. Instantly the alarm was raised and lithe horsemen came spurring out to meet him, guns in hand, faces tight and hostile. Although still weeks away from the Kansas railhead, the Pecos herd had already encountered localized hostility here north of the Panhandle.

The marshal's badge pinned to his lapel was in full view in the fading light as some six or seven horsemen closed in with wary aggression. The sight he made sobered them a little, for several Kansas lawmen had carved out fearsome reputations over the traildriving years, including in particular the recently appointed marshal of Chisum.

'You Jackman?' growled the first man, swinging his bronc around to fall in alongside.

'Yes.'

'What are you doin' out here?' demanded another.

'My job.'

They did not like his answer. A blocky man with the scarred face of trouble made to push his sweat-streaked cayuse in closer, but Jackman's cold eye checked him, held him to silence.

'I have business with Major McCord and I wouldn't advise anyone to interfere with it,' he stated flatly.

He had a way of delivering his words that had been

cultivated, honed and polished over the years. Complemented by his appearance and reputation, such words could often halt hotheads and hellions in their tracks, causing them to realize that they were likely encountering something way out of their depth. Such proved to be the case here on the rumpled plain as glances were exchanged and hurried whispered conversations hung in the air. Eventually a decision was reached. A path was cleared to enable the new arrival to continue on towards the camp unhindered, still under escort, yet with each rider ensuring he maintained a respectable distance.

There was no mistaking the cattleman. Harlen McCord stood tall and iron-jawed at the rear of his coach flanked by his trail boss and several riders sporting buckled guns. The cook and his sidekick broke off from ladling out son-of-a-gun stew to stare, and nobody in the hungry line-up complained.

Jackman was here.

The word that Chisum had taken the inflammatory step of importing a town-tamer of this status had first swept through the Pecos crew like a brush fire in August ten days earlier. The riders had been warned to expect trouble when they hit the streets of Chisum, but not even McCord had envisioned the new lawman daring to ride out to meet them here on their own turf, alone.

They respected few things as they did courage, this roughcase crew. What Jackman was doing smacked either of high courage or simple stupidity, nobody was sure which.

He reined in.

'Mr McCord, I believe?'

'You believe dead right, sir. And you would be the Gunner, I take it?'

A murmur washed through the rider ranks, striking a reaction. For 'the Gunner' had earned his soubriquet with his skill with the Colts, mainly against unruly mobs and frequently in trail towns. This was the new breed of Northern town-tamer they should recognize and detest on sight. A natural enemy. A gunman hiding behind a badge. Call him Hickok, Masterson, Earp, Holliday or Jackman – the profile was all too clear. Fast with a shooter, arrogant, pro-North and anti-Texan.

But they figured he must have courage aplenty, showing up out here all alone. Could this be some kind of trick? If so it was hard to see what shape it might take. Thirty of them, one of him, and not another Kansan in sight.

'I am the law,' he announced in a voice that carried. 'And the new law on the statute books of Chisum is that henceforth all north-bound herds and herders will continue on their way directly across the river without accessing the town. I'm told you are aware of this ordinance, sir, so I'd like to know your intentions. Do you intend to obey or will I deem you and your crew to be potential lawbreakers and treat you as such?'

'You sure have got gall for a cheap pistol-packing sonuva from the—' the cattle baron blurted.

'Cut it!' Jackman snapped. 'I'm not here to wrangle, simply to have your direct answer. I want that plainly stated and understood in the event of conflict and any deaths arising from your decision. Yes or no.'

McCord's broad face was tinged brick-red as he

lunged forward. The man had too long ruled all he surveyed in the vast regions of the Pecos. McCord manipulated the law in his own bailiwick, held it in contempt everyplace else.

'By God and by glory this so-called posting ordinance of theirs is nothing but a fraud and a fake. It was drawn up, not because of any threat we might pose but purely and simply because your dirty-fingered mayor is looking to rid himself of a rival for a woman he happens to be courting himself. Well, don't try and fake shock, Jackman. You know what I'm telling you is nothing but the truth.'

What Jackman did know, sitting his saddle and staring hard into this man's angry face, was that he had erred. He had not briefed himself fully on this party before accepting this assignment. Maybe he'd been too preoccupied with his own fitness and possibly the shock of meeting Carla again, to deploy his customary thoroughness.

And of course he was realizing fast that Carla was the main point of contention between the mayor of Chisum and the cattle boss of the Pecos.

He was still deliberating when movement caught his eye. He glanced west to sight two late-arriving cowboys outlined against the shimmering haze, coming in by the picket line.

These were no cowboys.

Despite troublesome eyesight, sifting dust and the refractions of the light, Jackman sensed instantly that these lithe silhouettes on horseback differed sharply from every other rider here. The way they sat their saddles, how their gun handles thrust outwards from lean hips, the very way they cut sharply around the tethered ponies to come trotting directly towards him, all combined in an instant to form a single impression: danger.

His reaction was lightning-fast. In a blur of movement impossible to follow, he whipped out his right-hand gun and had it cocked and levelled before anyone could do more than blink. The Thuer was trained squarely on Mac Tunney and Olan Quill, whose hawk features registered sudden alarm in the fading bronze glow of the sunset.

Only Jackman was aware that he was not seeing the men as sharply as he might have done a year, even six months, earlier.

'Hold it right there!' he commanded, his voice deep with outdoor authority. 'I am Marshal Jackman of Chisum and you will shuck your gunbelts, step down and walk here to me. Do it now!'

Nobody seemed to breathe. The major's top gunhawks had been with the herd from the outset. In that time Tunney and Quill had proved their mettle against Indians, rustlers and, in one bloody brush, with a raiding party of Comancheros in the Palo Duro region. Hard-working Pecos cowhands held the pair in something akin to awe, yet here was this Kansas lawman getting the drop on them and treating them like a couple of nobodies!

And Tunney and Quill seemed to be taking it!

This shocked the herders but came as no surprise to Jackman or the gunslicks themselves. For once the marshal had the drop, not even the gutsiest Pecos River gunslinger was about to risk going for iron just to prove he had the balls.

Gunrigs thudded to ground and the pair dismounted slowly. They came forward as though their hips had rusted up and they couldn't feel their legs any more.

Briskly, Jackman swung to ground, letting the reins dangle. He waited for the men to reach him. When they halted he deliberately drew the right skirt of his coat back and slid his Colt back into oiled leather, his eyes not leaving their faces for a moment.

'Tunney and Quill, right?'

They nodded, faces sullen, eyes alive with hate.

'Your boss made a big mistake hiring your kind. Without you, I'd treat everyone here just as saddle hands doing their job. But you make it different. The presence of hired shooters in this crew suggests that your employer is bent on mischief, perhaps out and out lawbreaking on Kansas soil. That won't be tolerated.'

'Finished?' McCord's face was livid.

'Before riding out today,' Jackman continued, 'I had it in my mind to have the board's posting ordinance withdrawn and invite you to visit my town, providing you respected the law. That is no longer on the cards, considering your presence. Instead, I'll enforce this regulation to the hilt. Chisum is hereby officially off limits to every Pecos herd rider.'

He turned his head to stare directly at the livid cattle king. 'That means every man from yourself down to the cook's louse, mister.'

He was offering the young guns every chance now. And they took it. He was still staring at McCord when he heard the sucked intake of breath, the rushing scrape of boot leather. Turning smoothly from the hips,

70

he confronted Quill and Tunney rushing at him with faces contorted and mouths snarling: a pair of savage bobcats ganging up on a larger predator.

It was an unwise move.

The marshal had set it up, and was ready. Barely seeming to shift his balance, he managed to evade Quill's clawing hands and sledged his left fist smack into the centre of the gunslinger's face. He felt the jarring shock of contact bolt up his arm and through his shoulder as Quill's fancy boots left the ground and he crashed flat on his back, sending up a great billow of bitter white dust.

Jackman ducked instinctively.

A fist whistled over his head and brushed the curve of his back. Tunney's momentum carried him into the marshal's jolting shoulder. Instantly Jackman pistoned his elbow into the man's solar plexus and Mac Tunney's face turned the colour of old pipeclay. Feebly he raised both fists protectively. Jackman drilled his right fist between them, putting every ounce of his 180 pounds behind it.

The Pecos' two finest lay head to toe upon the prairie grass, out to the world.

He stepped away, and still empty-handed and with hardly a hint of breathing heavily, started back for the grey. The sound of a dogie bawling for its momma sounded as loud as the triumphal roar of a hunting grizzly in the sucked-out silence as he fitted boot to stirrup and swung astride.

A combination of rage, hatred and twisted pride left the major trembling like a sick beast.

'You'll regret this, gunman!' he gritted through

71

locked teeth. 'Your stinking posting order is invalid under the constitution of the United States, as can be proved in any court of law. But even if that weren't the case I would not allow any two-bit gunman or jumped-up Jayhawker bar me from any place on this continent I want to go. Isn't that so, boys?'

A roar of assent came from thirty dusty throats as the marshal swung into his saddle and rode away. He'd said what he'd had to say with his fists. Next time, if needs be, he would back it up with his guns. It was up to McCord to decide if he wanted to buck the tiger or go on living.

CHAPTER 5

ALL OR NOTHING

Johnny Fallon grinned amiably and said: 'You should be jumping over the moon, Sheriff Latigo, you old scalp-lifter. Clay's put the stopper on the Pecos crew coming to town, which means you and Ash won't be up to your ears in bad-smelling waddies, and therefore you won't get treated like dirt like you were last year by those Brazos riders. So, howcome the long face, old-timer? Riddle me that.'

Few people treated Chisum's gruff old town sheriff this familiarly, but Johnny could always get away with it. The young man was regarded as an unpaid deputy here at the jailhouse, and indeed often stepped in to fill that role when trouble broke. At times this state of affairs worried Johnny's sister and she might be moved to dispatch Bowie to fetch him from the jailhouse and remind Johnny who paid his wages.

The half-breed Choctaw, who had watched Johnny grow over the years, often took him quietly aside to instruct him in how to handle himself. Johnny had proved a fast learner. If it was to do with peace-keeping, Johnny wanted to absorb it all.

Although Johnny regarded him as a pard, the husky 'breed didn't believe they could ever be that. Bowie's only friends were the same colour as himself. His way of handling the difficulties of the inter-racial complexities of the West he lived in now was to remain largely aloof from it all and keep his distance from white folks, something Johnny could never understand.

There were other things Carla Fallon's tall young brother didn't understand. Her involvement with a Texan rancher was one, her seeming indifference to Clay's reappearance another. He brought this latter matter up with Bowie on their way back to the saloon, and the man just looked at the sky in that way he had.

'Missy's got too much on her mind these days for me to worry about her and the marshal,' Bowie murmured. A group of Texans was making its way towards the Painted Lady on the opposite walk. Left over from earlier drives, they were drunk and noisy yet harmless. 'The marshal draws trouble wherever he goes whatever he does, I guess.'

'Are you bad-mouthing Clay again?' Johnny grinned.

The man smiled faintly.

'There you go again, Johnny. Nobody can say anything about the marshal to you.'

Johnny sobered and looked ahead.

'So OK, I rate Clay high. Why wouldn't I? I don't forget about how he carved up those hairy Cousin Jacks at Broken Bit the night they would've taken Sis's place apart, man. When you were laid up with your head in a sling, Clay was taking those bastards apart with his bare hands, or don't you remember?'

The 'breed just grunted. His loyalties went deep. He saw his mission in life as looking out for Carla Fallon. He had respect for the marshal, but at the same time saw him as a danger because of the fact that he suspected his mistress might still have feelings for the man.

There was nothing complicated about Bowie.

The cowboys mounted the porch and moved for the batwings between the blazing brands acting as torches. They glanced back at the two men following, then looked away, their manner subdued.

The imposition of the posting ordinance upon all future herds had had a sobering effect upon every rider from the South still in town.

The visiting Texans regarded the posting as high-handed and possibly unlawful, but were not saying so too loudly. They were waiting to see what befell the McCord herd, due in tomorrow, when the rancher realized that they were not welcome. That would be the test of the Board's new Jackman-backed policy, and until then, those enjoying Chisum's grudging hospitality were not about to raise any dust.

'I don't forget anything, Johnny,' Bowie replied, moving to straighten up one of his torches. 'I don't forget the good the marshal did that lousy town, nor the harm he did Miss Carla neither.'

'That was just one of those things that happen, *amigo*. Boy meets girl, boy and girl bust up. Happens every day.'

'It shouldn't happen to Miss Carla.'

'Old-timer, Sis is a woman like any other. These

things happen in life.'

'Whatever you say, Mr Johnny.'

'Don't close down on me, man,' Johnny said, leaning a hand against the saloon wall. He grinned. 'And think on this. You accuse me of holding Clay up as some kind of a hero. But what about you and Sis? She's the star in the east and the belle of the goddamn ball in your eyes.'

The 'breed scowled. Then he suddenly grinned. 'Guess you're right, Johnny. Anyways, better get inside. I think Miss Carla might have some chores waiting for you.'

'What else is new?' Johnny laughed easily and shouldered though the swinging doors, leaving Bowie to take up once again his position guarding his mistress's front doors against all dangers.

Inside, the professor seated himself at the Painted Lady's upright piano and began tinkling out a song about a dying cowboy and a big, bad painted blonde.

Johnny hit the street again at dusk, chores completed, his sister back in a good mood, the evening stretching invitingly ahead.

On the way to the courthouse-jailhouse complex he was aware of the tension Bowie had hinted at. Passing the Clayton House, he glimpsed Brawn Carter and Klegg Sands seated in a lamplit window of the dining-room, hitting the turtle soup. Rocking in a chair on the gallery was the agent for the McCord herd who had received the bad news just tonight that his outfit would be obliged to bypass the town which was now officially off limits.

No sign of anyone from the distant Pecos outfit as

76

yet, but Johnny sensed they would come. The last outfit had been smallish, but there was nothing minor about Harlen McCord and his crew. He shook his head in admiration of Clay Jackman in having the grit to ride out there alone, brace that big crew on its own turf and, according to reports, calling their bluff and pulling it off.

His grin faded as he raised the courthouse lights.

Of course some were already claiming that Clay was motivated by personal interests in his sister in posting the Pecos herd. Johnny doubted that. Clay and his sister had been all washed up by the time Jackman left Broken Bit, worse luck.

He believed Clay was simply doing his job with the herd, possibly didn't even know McCord had made a big play for Carla here last summer.

On reaching the courthouse he was obliged to take a seat and wait for the marshal to get through in what was now known as the show-up room.

Here the day's offenders were hauled in from the cells next door by the deputies, to be dealt with by Jackman just as Johnny had seen him do so often in Broken Bit.

The concept of the show-up room for offenders was Jackman's technique for making certain the public actually got to see the law being administered openly and properly. Under the bright lights above the judge's bench, now serving as the marshal's desk, any thief, wife-beater or rioting Texan herder could have his say, face his accusers and be dealt with fair, square and legal.

It had been said in other places that the town-tamer's

main reason in running his operations this way was to offset the perception of himself as simply a two-gun peace officer with no respect for the letter of the law, only for the kind of law that he might impose with a Colt full of bullets.

Johnny knew only too well that this had never been the case, as indeed did his sister. Jackman respected the letter of the law just as he accepted the fact that men like himself must be prepared to stand up against the gun hellions or see the law they respected falter and fail.

At Broken Bit, Johnny had been present at full trials which had resulted in badmen being found guilty, sentenced and hanged. There was little risk of anything of that nature here in Chisum as yet, for those being arraigned before the marshal tonight were not the great grey wolves of the wilderness or raging grizzlies. What Jackman's new net had gathered in over the past forty-eight hours were merely those vicious little alley cats, toothless predators who had been caught in simple snares, barking at changes in the weather.

Jackman permitted a Panhandler to leave without a fine, then glanced at the gallery to see Johnny there amongst the public, for whom these show-up room nights was a new free form of entertainment.

He nodded soberly and Johnny beamed proudly, glancing round to make sure everyone noted what a fine job the law-enforcer was doing. Johnny held Jackman in high regard, but even higher was his respect for the law. This obsession of his caused some people to dislike Carla Fallon's kid brother, but that didn't bother him any. Sis was about the most popular person in

Chisum, and he didn't even try to compete with that. Nor did he really wish to. He checked drunks, reminded citizens of their responsibilities and short-comings, and was always ready to back up the sheriff and his deputies. So there was no way he was ever going to be universally liked.

Which was just one further reason why he was so pleased that the winds of chance had blown Clay Jackman back into his life. Clay liked him – and Johnny refused to entertain the suspicion that this had anything to do with his sister. He and Chisum's city marshal were bona fide friends, and he would be proud of that fact no matter how it might annoy others.

Beneath the courtroom lights, Jackman squinted at the charge-book before him as the next offender was marched in by Sheriff Latigo. He found the lights of the courthouse far too bright for comfort. But their glare helped him get a good look at the short, ragged and unshaven character before him, who, before he was even made aware of the charges against him, blurted out his guilt and shame at having kicked his own wife down the rear landing steps of the Sagebrush Hotel while under the influence of the demon rum.

Jackman fined him five dollars and gave him another night in the cells.

So they kept coming tonight here in the trail town just as they had done in all the other places where he'd been hired to purge the troubled towns of their poison. Clean up the mean streets first before focusing on the fat men with big cigars who cooked up the crooked deals, cheated the poor, had a fat finger in every illegal pie.

No fat ones here tonight. Only the tricked, the trapped and the lost, perpetrators of small deeds furtively executed paraded past his big mahogany judge's bench tonight. These denizens of the back alleys neither howled nor rampaged, hatched no dark plots against men who wore badges on their vests. They were just the soft underbelly of boomtowns where big men were gathering up all they could hold in their fat fists – and the new marshal of Chisum dealt with them as such, sternly yet kindly.

And so he continued, until the last shuffling alley-bug was gone and he was at last able to signal for the lights to be doused. He put thumb and forefinger to the inner corners of his eyes and held them there until the voice sounded at his elbow.

'You OK, Clay?'

'Sure, Johnny boy. You eaten yet?'

'No sir, but we're about to. Right?'

'Damn right.'

It had been a long and testing day but the marshal of Chisum was feeling fine as they headed for Midge Griddle's diner on the corner. He and Carla's brother had always hit it off. He'd cultivated and enjoyed the youngster's friendship years ago, but somehow it meant even more here. For one thing, Johnny was now a man and showed a remarkable interest in the law. But for another, his was a genuinely friendly face in a place that might respect him but certainly would not presume to show friendly towards a man of his sternness and reputation.

So the kid had something rare from the lawman's point of view. When he looked at Johnny Fallon he saw unquestioning affection and loyalty in his eyes. For a man who walked virtually all streets alone, this honest and undemanding friendship supplied something he had missed, something he was pleased to have found again.

Even a man who stood as tall as the marshal, the terror of the wild Texans and nemesis to lawbreakers everywhere, needed at least one genuine friend. Offhand, he could not think of one other.

The board meeting being held behind closed doors at the old council chambers building on Aimes Street was not going well. It was felt by some that Mayor Klegg Sands had acted hastily in authorizing Marshal Jackman to enforce the posting ordinance, which had immediately been effected on three small herds on the plains. And, of course, on a fourth. Namely, the large outfit from the Pecos due to cross the river in just a few days' time.

They should have been consulted, Mayor Sands was told. Members with business interests and commitments should have been given fair warning before Jackman was dispatched to inform the incoming Texans that their trade was no longer desired or required.

How would they survive now without the heavy input from the trail herds? After all, had not Sands and others created Chisum originally for the specific purpose of attracting the herds and thereby siphoning off some of the money and business involved before the herds reached the Kansas railroads?

Klegg Sands would not deny it.

But times had changed, he insisted, up on his feet

now and fairly bristling with conviction. It was time for the town to graduate and come of age. Fortunes had been made, certainly, yet the costs had been high. 'Just go take a look at the size of our graveyard if any of you have any doubts about that!' Last year they'd had a sheriff shot and killed and a section of town below the Deadline burned as the result of a riot involving Texans. And this year the board had been obliged to dig very deep to secure the services of a high profile town-tamer merely to maintain everyday law and order. Wasn't that a sign that it was time to call a halt, reject the herd trade now and see the town stand on its own feet, independent of the Texans?

'But that's just the point, Klegg,' objected the lantern-jawed realtor. 'In the short time he's been here, Marshal Jackman has imposed the very kind of order we've been craving from the first.' He spread his hands. 'Why choose this year to shoot our milch cow just when we've finally got it to behave itself?'

Murmurs of approval greeted these words. Why indeed? Overnight, Jackman had virtually stopped public brawling, horse-racing in the streets and any sort of serious outbreak beyond the Deadline. The marshal might well be a tad grim and inaccessible but none could deny he was working even better than they might have hoped. Why change at such a propitious time?

'Because we are able to change now,' Sands emphasized. 'Until we had a man of the marshal's calibre at the helm there was simply no way we could enforce our posting ordinance. We did not have that capability. We could have nailed it up on the post office wall and the cowboys would have torn it up and lighted their cigarettes with it. Before we could impose our laws on others we had to ensure we had the capability to do so. Surely that is plain enough?'

It was silent for a time in the long, smoke-filled room as merchants, dealers, proprietors and entrepreneurs moodily considered the realtor's words. It might well be true that the possibility of one day posting the town off limits to the hellraising herders had been on the board's books for two years now. Yet many had never thought they would actually ever get round to imposing it. Sands's precipitate action had taken them by surprise, and more than one townsman harboured a suspicion that there might be an ulterior reason for his so doing.

It was left to the stage-line owner to get at last to his feet and pronounce in plain words this nagging concern for Mayor Sands's benefit.

'Mr Mayor, is it or ain't it true that what drove you to sic Jackman on to McCord is the fact that the Texican has made it public that he aims to woo and wed Miz Fallon this summer iffen it's the last thing he does? And I guess it's just as reliable a fact of life that everyone here knows how you feel about her yourself, so. . . .'

The speaker allowed his words to ebb away and a congealing silence spread as every eye in the room focused on Klegg Sands in his chair at the head of the table.

You could hear the quiet.

Then the mayor was on his feet. 'If you're implying I'm motivated by personal reasons then you are badly mistaken, Walker,' he intoned. Thinking: *I'll transfer all my shipping business from him to the opposition first thing*

tomorrow, and I'll have his seat on the board inside the week.
A pause. 'As always I have only the town's good at heart
and nothing will convince me that what I've done will
not prove to be for the overall good of the town we all
believe in.'

'I second and support the mayor.'

The speaker on his feet was Brawn Carter, saloonkeeper and Sands stooge. His interjection and support
spelt the end to all resistance. Sands had the power and
that power had been enforced. Seemed there was very
little to be said now until that oddity at board meetings,
a guest, stubbed out his cigar in a brass tray and rose to
his rawboned six-three looking anything but concilia-
tory. The trail boss of the Buckley herd had demanded
to be allowed to sit in but was far from impressed.

The man had harsh things to say and they allowed
him to say them.

They were raindrops on a duck's back. Carter and
Sands lighted up cigars and two members began a whispered conversation.

It wasn't long before the trail boss reddened,
grabbed up his hat and strode to the doors.

'All right, let the decision be on your own heads,' he
thundered. 'We'll see if you are so damn smug when Mr
McCord decides what is to be done about your damned
ordinance. Us? We're headin' on, and be damned to
you. And when we hit Dodge City you can be sure we'll
be lettin' every Texan know where you stand and what
a bunch of dung-eatin' Jayhawker bloodsuckers you are
down here.'

'I hear tell Dodge is clamping down on you Texans
also,' interjected the stock agent, who handled a lot of

the shipping details.

'Then the hell with Dodge City too!' snorted this angry man from Wichita Falls. 'They are cut from the same greedy cloth as you up there, always were. So, Greensburg will get our business, and you can wager we won't be the only ones headin' there. And that'll trim your sails too, Sands, as I happen to know you got interests up there as well. I hope you all go broke – that's if the Pecos boys don't run you up a tree first.'

He was gone, the crash of the slamming door threatening to jolt the framed pictures of the mayor from the walls.

But Klegg Sands only smiled behind a curtain of cigar smoke. 'Sore loser. Typical brushpopper.'

'You reckon he'll ship at Greensburg?' enquired a man who had a business in Chisum.

Sands shrugged.

'Two hundred head? Who gives a toss? Brawn, I think we should have a little drink to celebrate our final coming of age. I would like to drink a toast to Chisum's future as a centre of trade and commerce and civic administration as opposed to being little more than one big saloon and whorehouse for people we hate anyway. I trust you'll all be drinking with me, my friends?'

Everyone drank that toast, and the general consensus now seemed to be: if the mayor says it will work out, why should we worry?

Brawn Carter suddenly dropped the whiskey decanter and hit the floor when a window exploded at his back and a rock the size of a cantaloupe bounced off the oak table.

85

'Jayhawker vermin!' came the shout from the street, and a second rock slammed into a wall and shattered with a noise like a gunshot.

Sands alone strode to the window to stare out. Directly across the street stood a bunch of men in Levis and big hats. He identified the rawboned Chisolm trail boss amongst them. The mayor shook his fist and shouted. This did not deter a man he identified as Bad Ethan from scooping up a half-brick and letting fly.

The wild waddy's aim was bad but his velocity was impressive as the door shuddered under the impact.

'We're gonna tree your stinkin' town and take it over, you Kansan scum!' Bad Ethan raged, and was clawing at the gun on his hip when two men swung into the lamp-light from Clover Alley, hard by the City Billiard Parlour.

The taller of the two was the marshal. Immediately, a smiling Mayor Sands invited his cowering fellow board members to come take a look at the living proof that their money was being well spent.

Not even Brawn Carter suspected that Clay Jackman himself was on Sands's hate list, and would be dealt with just as soon as the Texan troubles were resolved. At heart Klegg Sands was a taker and would not quit until he had his fists wrapped around everything. The money, the town, the power and the woman. The whole pot.

He smiled and drew deeply on his cheroot as they watched the marshal shoulder Bad Ethan clear off the walk to land on his head in the street with a sickening crunch.

CHAPTER 6

RIOT NIGHT

'Take him!' bawled the rawboned trail boss, snatching up a chair from the porch close by. 'Git the varmint afore he can bring them hoglegs into play, boys. He cain't do Ethan that way.'

The waddies showed willing. Fanning wide, they came at the marshal from three sides as he moved nimbly to get his back against the front wall of the City Billiard Parlour. Watching intently from in back of the Chisolm bunch, Johnny Fallon let loose with a shout at the top of his lungs. 'Cut loose, Clay! Show them how it's done. Show them how we handled Broken Bit!'

But Jackman's hands remained empty as the semicircle of danger closed in. Empty but clenched. He appeared to be smiling in the shadow of his hat, but it was hard to tell. The first waddy drew within range and was winding up a haymaker when a polished boot flashed out and cracked his kneecap. As the man howled and hopped away, Jackman drove forward to shoulder-charge the bow-legged waddy while he was

87

diverted by his companion's yelps of agony.

A dazed Bad Ethan just managed to make it to his feet when Bandy crashed into him, both men tumbling to ground in a wild tangle of arms and legs.

Two cowboys erupted from the rapidly swelling ring of onlookers, liquored-up and loaded for bear. The marshal was their target but they didn't make it. Suddenly Augie Gee was there, grinning in that foolish way he had, but swinging like a gate. One man went down under his first punch. The other veered away from Jackman, lowered his head like a ram, charged. With the skill of a matador, Augie swayed smoothly aside then brought his knee snapping up under an unshaven jaw as the big brawler charged by. There was a sound like an axe biting wet wood and the man went staggering blindly into the circle of onlookers bringing three of them down with as he finally crashed to ground, out to the world.

'Good man, Augie!' Johnny shouted, then ducked nimbly as a haymaker whistled close.

Jackman saw that punch miss, then had troubles of his own as others closed in on him, unshaven faces grim and determined. But he was ready for them. Still no guns. No indecision, uncertainty or concerns about eyesight either. Jackman suddenly felt free as a hunting wolf and just as dangerous. He was the law, these were the lawless, and no situation could get any simpler than that. Right now, he felt impelled not to resort to the guns but to have the enemy feel the impact of a more personal power.

His fists were grenades and they exploded against jaws, cheekbones and noses in a succession of lightning blows that put another two off the walk and dropped another man to his knees.

Jackman was calmly waiting for the trail boss, who was holding a heavy chair over his head with murderous intent, to reach him, when something blurred past him and Johnny Fallon dived headlong at the Chisolm man and hit him like a pile-driver.

The descending chair shattered across Johnny's back. The youngster grunted as he hit the floorboards, but was rising swiftly to go on with it when Jackman joined the party. His shoulder caught the chair-swinger squarely in the chest to slam him backwards with such force that he snapped off an awning support on his way to the street where he landed like a sack of meat.

As the marshal regained his balance, Bad Ethan regained the plankwalk in back of him.

This forward scout of the Pecos herd had earned his nickname honestly. A man of medium height, average appearance and a genuinely evil temper, this one was a back-alley brawler from the hard rock country. And he always fought dirty.

A savage blow caught Jackman from behind. The lawman staggered and Bad Ethan rushed to follow up his advantage. Too late. Johnny got between the two men first. Two vicious straight rights smashed bones in the brawler's face. Johnny then seized a dangling arm, slung the man over his back and heaved him bodily into the street where he crashed against the water-trough with a sickening thud.

Someone cheered as a nimble Augie jumped upon the unconscious man's back, then grinning and excited, held clenched fists aloft in triumph.

As others fell back in awe, two late-arriving drunks chimed in. As Johnny sparred with a red-headed swinger, Jackman shook his head clear and attacked. He stopped his man dead in his tracks with a vicious head-butt; no Queensberry rules in this ruckus. Crimson splashed and the man stumbled blindly into the wall, then fell flat on his back, whimpering like a baby.

The red-headed roughcase veered away from Clay and attempted to headbutt Johnny. Augie stuck out a boot, causing the man to stumble. Lightning-quick, Johnny pistoned his knee into the man's guts. He threw up as he was falling and Johnny hastened his way to the boards with a rabbit-killer to the base of the neck that caused him to hit face first, bouncing from the impact.

The end came when a half-recovered Bad Ethan clambered back up on the gallery and charged into what was left of the mêlée, slobbering and half-blinded with blood, yet still dangerous. Clay suddenly feigned injury and slumped at the knees, dropping his hands. Eagerly, Bad Ethan rushed in for the knockout. At the last moment Clay 'came to', seized the man around the knees, lifted him bodily and hurled him back into the street where he landed with a sickening thud.

In the same moment, Johnny stopped the last wild swinger in his tracks with a left to the point, followed up by a looping right hook which caught the jaw square, mashing the big ganglion of nerves there, causing his adversary to lose all sensation in arms and legs as he thudded to his knees, knuckles dragging on the boards and his tongue lolling like a big dog's.

Almost gently, the panting Jackman toed the brawler off the porch into the street, then at last hauled his right-hand Thuer conversion Colt.

Only to find he didn't need it.

The Chisolm crew had made their big play but hadn't been good enough to see it through. They were all done.

Jackman was feeding a grinning Johnny and Augie Gee rye from his hip-flask when Sands and Carter arrived upon the scene. The mayor of Chisum and his sidekick from the board did not take it kindly when ordered by Jackman to go find medical assistance for the battered rioters, although this raised murmurs of both appreciation and amusement from a section of the crowd.

Sands seemed ready to object until Jackman repeated his order. Standing there in the lamplight the town-tamer appeared totally intimidating. It suddenly seemed more prudent to respond than argue, which was exactly what the board members did. Quickly and without comment.

Having recovered his hat, which had been dislodged in the fight, Clay quietly instructed the mob to escort all mobile Chisolm riders beyond the city limits. There would be no arrests. He insisted that the cowboys were basically harmless, had learned their lesson and would not give any more trouble before collecting their cows and heading up for Greensburg.

By the time the street was cleared without further incident, and the last rioter had ridden out with his tail between his legs, even the marshal's critics and enemies began to wonder if this might not be the rarest breed there was; the man who seemed incapable of making a mistake or putting a foot wrong.

*

The herd had not moved one mile in forty-eight hours.
The tail-end of a norther had swept across the plains
overnight. But although the day was clear and bright,
there was mud underfoot and McCord had needed to
shift his coach and tent to higher ground, from which
point he could survey the grazing sea of red backs, the
plains reaching to the north and, in the far distance
northwards, the chimney-smoke and the glitter of
sunlight on the metal raincatchers of the distant town
across the faint blue trace of Burnt River. Now, seated
behind a folding table in a sturdy camp-chair like a
commander in the field, the big man did a deal of both
smoking and thinking. He occasionally consulted with
his leading hands and received a number of communications.

One such of interest that morning was to do with the
Chisolm herd's decision to ship from Greensburg after
being turned away from Chisum. Another message
from their trail agent in Chisum informed that another
two minor herds had also been moved on and likewise
had chosen Greensburg as their destination in preference to Dodge or Wichita.

But it was the third communication, on scented
paper and written in a fine familiar hand, that brought
the cattleman out of his camp-chair and spitting out
what remained of his cigar.

Miss Fallon was cordial and expressed regrets at the
turn of recent events, but really did believe it would be
best were the major to abide by the posting ordinance
and bypass Chisum, despite his intentions to visit her as

they had discussed in previous communications.

Suddenly he felt the need of a drink, and promptly slammed down three fingers of straight rye. He did not even cough.

As he rested the knuckles of his right hand on the table, Harlen McCord's weathered, square-jawed Texas face was a study.

He was a man accustomed to getting what he wanted. Whenever he saw something he desired, he considered, formulated his plans then put them into action, and almost always came away with whatever prize might have caught his eye.

He had already become the biggest beef-raiser in the Pecos region this time last year, when he'd rolled north with his Dodge-bound herd of primes. He was a war hero, cattle king and still very much in his prime at fifty years of age. He thought he had everything he really desired until he happened to walk into the Painted Lady in Chisum late one night, to meet the woman of his dreams.

The fact that Carla Fallon seemed to treat the major no better or worse than any number of admirers didn't faze him a bit. He'd set out to break down her resistance with letters and presents during the long winter months, and was eventually rewarded with at least some signs of interest over a two-month stopover in Chisum before he left for the Pecos again.

He disregarded reports that wealthy Klegg Sands was also keenly pursuing the Painted Lady's lovely owner. Carla was all class, and McCord contended that, despite his suaveness and wealth, the mayor of Chisum was a dog.

By contrast, McCord's aristocratic family reached back three generations. And what he might lack in some social graces he believed he more than made up for in other directions.

With one failed childless marriage in back of him, the hero of the Civil War was ready to remarry and begin a dynasty, had believed himself to be firmly on course for that goal before running into an unexpected obstacle out here on the Panhandle plains.

The guntipper.

They could call Jackman whatever they liked, he was still just another Kansan gunslinger in the major's eyes. Hell, they even called him the Gunner, and the name apparently fitted him like a glove.

The Gunner and the mayor. That was the double threat awaiting him on the Kansan border, and McCord berated himself for not having anticipated trouble of some similar nature beforehand.

He broodingly considered Mayor Sands of Chisum.

The man was wealthy and powerful and owned half Chisum, likely would not rest until he held the whole place in his clenched fist.

As he saw it, Sands had first cast his wandering eye upon Carla Fallon, then discovered he had a rival in Texas. His guess was that, under the pretext of bringing order to his streets, the mayor had shipped in Jackman and promptly made full use of him to enforce the posting ordinance barring him from both the city and the woman he wanted to marry.

The devious bastard!

But McCord's challenges did not end there.

While he'd never considered Sands a serious rival for

the woman's affections, Jackman was plainly a horse of a very different colour, and it had come as a body blow for McCord to discover that the town-tamer and Carla had been lovers in the past.

And lastly, the big man was genuinely jealous. For Jackman was as impressive a specimen as he had seen, younger than himself and a legend, even if an unsavoury one to many eyes. Carla might protest that all that lay in the past. Yet what was he to make of the report that Jackman and her brother had spent the entire day at the Painted Lady the day after their big street fight with the wild boys?

The major sniffed.

There was a stink in the air here and he knew what it was. The stench of Kansas. He'd fought the bastards during the War, his father had always referred to them as the 'turncoat, dirt-farmer scum of the West,' and every Texican worth his salt had cause to hate their guts. And now Kansan had connived with Kansan to humiliate and defeat Harlen McCord of Pecos Ranch, and could conceivably cost him the the woman he was convinced he loved. He was being treated like an alien in his own country and they would have him believe that the law supported their actions.

And they honestly believed that he would simply sit back and take that?

How loco could you get!

Another rider skirted the herd and loped up the rise. The latest word from Chisum was that the Dunstan herd had crossed the river, heading for Greensburg without stopping over at Chisum and without even seeking to test the strength of the posting ordinance.

It was testament to his will power that for some time after receiving that piece of news, McCord was able to concentrate upon necessary correspondence and matters to do with the herd.

Upon emerging from his big Sibley tent he was surprised to find that Mac Tunney and Olan Quill had ridden in. The pair were now seated side by side on the wagon tongue of his coach, soaking up the sun and puffing on Durham cigarettes.

The gunmen rose together and right away McCord smelt something in the air. The two were dressed in the dapper flashy way they affected in order to distinguish themselves from rough-garbed herders with dung on their boots. Oiled gunrigs and leather gleamed in the light and the dark bruise marks on the faces of both men were slowly fading. The pair appeared neat, compact and sure of themselves as usual, but this didn't explain what was different about them.

They waited for him to approach before Quill flicked his butt away and stamped on it.

'We're going into town, boss,' he announced quietly.

'That's against my orders,' McCord responded.

'Sorry,' Tunney drawled. 'But like Olan says, we are riding into Chisum, whether you or that long nosed badgeman says so or not.' He hooked his thumbs in his shell-belt and slipped into the classic, feet-apart gunman's challenging stance. 'A cowman with no cows ain't a cowman, boss man. Same goes for a man of the gun. Without respect, he ain't no gunman. When the Gunner jumped us, he took our respect off of us. Now we are riding in to grab it back.'

'Just felt you ought to know, Mr McCord,' supported the other.

'If we don't get back for any reason—'

'Hold up, hold up, damnit! Give me a minute!' McCord cut in.

The gunmen exchanged quizzical glances. They didn't speak as McCord clambered up on to the high seat of his coach and seated himself, facing north. He sat detached and remote with a strange cold current flowing through him. He knew now that he could not buckle under. Would not. Understanding came like that to this Texan.

A man lived with danger in the West. You accepted it as one of the conditions of staying here instead of seeking some safe, secure nook for yourself back East. Sometimes ambition or lust might dull the edge of a Texan's courage and pride. But a man never really lost it. Something always brought you back to it, and in this instance it was just the pride-driven resolution of a couple of lethal men young enough to be his sons that did the trick.

He rose suddenly and jumped down from the high seat, something he had not done in a long time. He was pleased with the way he landed. There was plenty juice in his fifty-years-old joints yet.

He looked Tunney and Quill in the eye. 'Maybe you'd appreciate some company?'

The fight at the cathouse was short-lived. The drummer from Coleyville had started in pushing one of the girls around, the madam hollered for the law, and, as bad luck would have it for the love-bandit drummer, the

marshal happened to be just several doors away inter-
rogating a suspect in a case of petty theft.

The offender went to water when Jackman's long
shadow fell through the doorway, was ready to give
himself up and take what was coming to him. Arrest,
appearance in tonight's show-up and maybe a five-spot
fine would seem the appropriate punishment. Instead
the marshal poleaxed the man with his pistol barrel and
threw him out into the yard for the towel boy to tend to
while the grateful madam poured the badgeman a shot.

'Everything OK with you, Marshal?' She was a faded
Southern ante-bellum belle with golden ringlets and
highly rouged cheeks. It sent a tremor through her
worn-out old hooker's heart to have a man of such style
and stature ornamenting her plush parlour, and she
batted her eyelashes and oozed a waft of attar of roses
in his direction as he occupied her best chair. 'You
seem a little tense.'

Jackman stared at the woman, for a long moment
looking every inch the man he was expected to be in
this town. The iron lawman, unfriendly, uncompromis-
ing and certainly no friend of citizens like her or those
who frequented her place of business.

Next moment he was looking about for someplace to
sit down. It had been a long hard day, and such days
sometimes caused him to feel as though he was about to
cave in, like a man made of straw.

A hand was on his elbow and the madam guided him
unprotestingly across the parlour and through a doorway hung with purple drapes and strung beads which
tinkled. This was Madam's private office. There was a
chair by the window, a bottle on the desk. It was as if she

instinctively realized his needs, his moment of weakness. The Gunner had to admit he felt grateful as he leaned back against that soft leather with the glass in his fingers and slanted sunlight cutting across his knees. A fat black cat stared across at him curiously from the chaise longue.

'You can relax here, Mr Jackman. Take your gunbelt off. Put your eyeglasses on if you want.'

'What? What eyeglasses?'

'Hey, you're in here and not out there on those crummy streets now,' Madam drawled, lighting up a Turkish cigarette. Here in her own little domain the woman seemed to shed her glitzy public persona and assumed a natural, world-weary dignity, as though it was not bordello keeper and marshal any longer, just a couple of weary people taking a break from all that reality lurking beyond the purple drapes. She sat down, crossed her legs and gusted smoke at the ceiling. 'You don't see good but you don't dast wear your glasses for fear of what folks might say. The jokes. Yet you tote them round. That bulge in your fine jacket just under that big old badge, that's your eyeglasses as anybody with one eye could see. Go ahead, Mr Jackman. Put 'em on. I won't split on you.'

He stared.

It was in him to react as anyone who knew him might expect. As he'd reacted instinctively to any who dared try and penetrate the armour of invincibility he'd clothed himself in twenty years ago, and never shucked off.

But he didn't.

Suddenly it felt real good to have someone level with

him and talk to him like a man, not someone you had to treat with kid gloves, as though he were something special, or worse, dangerous.

For despite his somewhat arrogant street manner with which the wild towns were familiar, Jackman was neither vain nor naturally cold. What they saw out there was what he'd fashioned himself into in order to survive. He had to look, act and appear bigger than the next man in order to impress and be able to exert his authority, otherwise every bum, gun-punk and woolly-headed cowpoke would be trying to take him down every time he walked upon the street.

Almost defiantly, he set his glass aside and took out the metal spectacle case from his inside jacket pocket. He extracted the glasses, put them on and was immediately able to see that her eyes were grey, not blue. That she was even more worn by the years, yet oddly more attractive, than he'd imagined.

The flowers in the vase, the clean line of the sunbeams coming through the window, the patch of turquoise sky – all were suddenly vivid and sharply etched.

'How old are you, Mr Jackman?'

He actually grinned. Plainly no point in his reacting against her impertinence and curiosity now they had gone this far. She would just see right through him anyway.

'Forty-one. And, yes, I'm too old for this work and my eyesight's not what it used to be. Anything else?

'So, why don't you quit?'

'It's what I do.'

'There are other jobs. You're smart. You look good.

Seems to me a man like you could do 'most anything he set his mind to.'

Jackman sipped his malt whiskey. From the street the low rumble of traffic sounded just right to his ear. Chisum was drowsing through a quiet hour. It would change eventually, of course. But for the moment it was good to be removed from it all. Real good.

'A lady like yourself must have heard all the stories,' he said quietly. 'Mine might be a tad different from the general run but not all that remarkable.' He stared down at his glass. The whiskey was rich amber. 'Born poor, little education, no prospects better than riding, mining, whatever. But I was good with a gun and I surely disliked seeing good people get pushed around. So I parlayed all that into my first peace-keeping job and stayed at it. End of story.'

'They'll kill you if you don't quit.'

'Seems to me I'd die if I quit. What would I do? Stand behind a counter selling groceries? Go trailing or hunting and sleep in the open at over forty? This is all I know how to do.'

'What about Miss Fallon?'

'What?'

'Spare me the surprise, Marshal. Someone like me hears everything sooner or later, and I heard all about you and the lady from the saloon days ago.'

'Just what did you hear?'

'That you was close once. That she's been carrying a torch for you ever since. That Sands hates your guts because he's sweet on her too. He hired you not knowing Carla Fallon prefers her menfolk tall and kinda grim to shifty-eyed money-shufflers like him. I know

McCord the Texican lost his head over the same lady, and that he won't be posted from the town by you or a dozen like you. Hell, I could go on all day about what I know. But why bother? What it all adds up to is that if you stay on here wearing that there badge and playing God and bracing every man who looks at you crosswise, you could wind up in deeper trouble than you've been anyplace before. When all you really want is to hang up those shooting-irons, leave them spectacles on your nose and find yourself some kind of life where you might live to see fifty, sixty even.'

He removed his glasses, finished his drink, rose and picked up his hat.

'Is that it?' he asked.

'No good you trying to play your strong silent part with me again now, Mr Jackman,' she said with a crooked smile. 'Not after you've already opened the door on yourself and let me look in.'

She rose and placed a hand upon his arm.

'I'm ten years older than you and I'm still doing the only thing I ever knew, just like you. I'm also alone and will be till I die, as nobody marries an old whore. My work might be pretty low, but it won't kill me. Seems to me you're going to have to bend some along the way or you'll never see a kid of your own born, let alone ever have a grandson to dandle on your knee.'

He'd never had a conversation quite like this before. He found it both revelatory and deeply disturbing. The madam was forcing him to strip everything else away and consider reality. But maybe he was not ready for that yet. Maybe he would never be.

The little room was still. Dust motes danced in the

sunbeams. Upstairs a floorboard creaked and the marshal of Chisum found himself listening for the sounds of the street that were not there.

'What. . . ?' the woman said as she too sensed the unnatural quiet. She started for the window but his voice halted her.

'Don't bother.' He fitted his hat to his head, just so. 'That sort of quiet only ever means the one thing, Madam. Trouble.' His smile was grim. 'See what I mean about me and my job? It's what I know and all I know.'

She said nothing as he left. She didn't even go to the window. Whatever it might be out there, the madam did not want to see.

CHAPTER 7

FALLEN IDOL

'Here he comes!' someone shouted.

All along the central block they heard the shout – the drinkers on the saloon porches, the small crowd of nervous citizens clustered around the fountain and the matrons who had sought refuge at the Ladies' Auxiliary when the riders first appeared. All craned their necks to catch a glimpse of the man they had been waiting to see for what seemed an eternity yet was in reality but a handful of minutes.

So recent in fact had been the Pecos riders' illegal crossing of the town perimeter that the dust of their coming was still sifting back down out of the sky over rooftop, carbarn, false-front and street.

And both those children in respectable attire and the street urchins with their patched pants who peered out through railings and from alley-mouths, were wondering why all the adults were acting so strangely. For few, if any, were as yet aware of the tension in the air that every adult could feel, both heavy and menacing.

Above them upon the up-a-flight balcony of one of his offices, Klegg Sands's gaze encompassed the scene, watching over it as though it were all his creation, which to a great degree it was. What was going on behind Mr Big's opaque gaze as he stood barbered and tailored alongside hulking Brawn Carter, there was no telling. But faces kept glancing at the two men as they did at the sheriff, visible across the street, framed in the jail-house doorway.

For while the marshal was the man who'd delivered the posting order to the herd camped beyond the river, it had been entirely the creation and handiwork of mayor and sheriff.

In sharp contrast to his employer the mayor, Sheriff Latigo was leaking nervous sweat in the hot slanting sunshine which cast a dusty golden glaze over everything it touched. Possibly the sheriff was recalling the fate of his predecessor the last time the Texans menaced the town of Chisum.

That this was some kind of similar defiant stand there was little doubt, and worried eyes still searched in vain for a glimpse of their formidable town-tamer now.

Jackman's visit to the Pecos herd had received wide publicity over the intervening forty-eight hours, and by now almost everyone understood its purpose.

Harlen McCord had been officially advised that neither he, his men nor his cattle were any longer free under law to come within ten miles of the town limits.

Yet they had already come.

The Pecos cattle baron who stood by his gleaming coach-and-pair directly out front of the town hall was in full view of every citizen, and had been for some time

105

now. Mace Street was by this almost blocked off by more than twenty grim and gun-hung Texans, sitting their saddles or lounging by the hitch racks. Invading herders, like the citizens, were puzzled to know why the marshal's appearance had been announced so confidently and dramatically, yet there was still no sign of him.

Was it possible the Gunner had made a quick appraisal of the tense situation and maybe forked a fast horse?

Nobody really believed that. Jackman's rule had been so dramatic and authoritative over recent weeks that not even his enemies were prepared to give that hypothesis a moment's serious consideration. Even the two ragged urchins perched skinny-legged atop water-barrels in Wagon Alley seemed positive that this show – whatever kind of puzzling, grown-ups' drama it might prove to be – would not proceed without the tall man in brown.

'My dad says the marshal ain't afraid of no Texan born, Jimmy. You reckon he might shoot someone today?'

'Well, he shot all them fellers on that train, didn't he? Twenty or thirty, wasn't there?'

'But there must be a hundred Texans down yonder. Could he shoot that many?'

'Heck, he's shot a lot more'n that already.'

'You sure of that?'

'Just as sure that I ain't gonna miss none of it . . . but where is he anyways?'

Half a block south of Wagon Alley stood Mother Malloy's hat shop, all chintz curtains and tasteful gold-leaf lettering on the plate-glass windows.

Behind the windows, Clay Jackman stood talking quietly with Carla and Johnny Fallon with Mother Malloy and Bowie the 'breed silent in the background.

There were tears in Carla's eyes now and her brother was growing tense. Sheer chance had found the Fallons at the shop when Jackman rounded the corner from Holly Street into Mace, on his way to face down the invaders. Immediately Johnny had rushed out to offer his assistance, and it was only then that Clay had sighted Carla standing the doorway with alarm clouding her face.

He was now trying to convince her that the situation was not as dire as it might appear before continuing on to do what he must. Everyday stuff for any lawman, he insisted. Hadn't she witnessed confrontations like this in Broken Bit, and hadn't he handled every one?

He sounded cool and understated. Yet just the sight of her tears was like a knot in his guts. The madam and their strange conversation was still fresh in his mind. She'd said things nobody had said to him in years, had caught him at a rare moment of weakness and uncertainty and capitalized on it.

That woman had planted seeds of doubt in his mind. Some had lingered.

There was a shadow of reluctance in the marshal's mind that shimmering, heat-stricken afternoon, and this scene was doing nothing to dispel it.

He glanced at Carla, her tears.

That was what was doing the real damage. Sure, he'd always known she had not stopped caring for him, as he still did for her. Yet she was reacting to this situation just as she had done back in Broken Bit when they'd been lovers. What was he to make of that?

He had to be clear in his mind in order to work efficiently, yet instead he felt confused.

He'd believed they had buried whatever had once been between them in Broken Bit a long time ago. But why the tears? And shouldn't she be more concerned about McCord anyway? The Texan was her suitor, perhaps Sands also. He was just someone she had known once. And he had not changed for the better. He had been the Gunner then and was still so today. Nobody should weep for men like him.

'Carla, I want you to go back to the Lady right now,' he said firmly. 'All of you. I'll settle this and be along once I've dealt with th—'

'Damnit, Clay, the Texans have got their gunsharks with them,' protested Johnny, his pale face alive with excitement and concern. 'Quill and Tunney. They rode right by this door earlier, looking mean as poison. You're going to need backing. You know you can count on me.'

Jackman was impressed, yet frowned dismissively. He threw a glance at Bowie whose bronzed face was an expressionless mask. The 'breed was detached, unemotional and uninvolved. That suited the marshal. Times like this he preferred to be one-out. The badge-toter versus the mob. It had always been that way, would be again here today.

'Take them home,' he ordered Bowie roughly. 'Go the back way and keep moving.'

Carla reached for him but Clay was already gone.

The glare off the street struck his eyes but his only

108

response was to tug his hatbrim an inch lower as he lengthened his stride, walking at a medium long-legged pace down the dead centre of the empty street like an actor playing an all too familiar role yet again.

The scene at the hat-shop no longer existed. Once again the years of discipline had come to his aid and he was complete. And as his clearing gaze fixed upon the mass of the mob some distance ahead, so dark against the hot white of the street, he was not seeing a score of adversaries so much as just one.

Virtually every mob had its nucleus around which the lesser atoms and molecules buzzed furiously. You always went for the nucleus. And it didn't surprise Clay Jackman one iota to realize that he was calmly prepared to take out his sixguns and blow the hero of the war and pride of the Pecos straight into hell if that was what it took.

That was simply his job. It was what he did.

Not a single eye was able to unhook itself from his tall, lean figure as he cut the distance to the town hall from a hundred yards to fifty. The sudden sharp clatter of a kid tumbling off a water-barrel in Wagon Alley caused onlookers to start, yet had no apparent effect on the marshal nor the men he found himself facing when he eventually turned the haberdasher's corner, where he drew to a halt.

His cold stare focused momentarily upon the powerful, defiant figure of the cattleman standing by the coach, but his gaze swiftly flickered away to see and assess the Pecos fire-power.

The cattle drive's hired guns leaned indolently against a hitch rail which thrust at an angle out from the general store hard by Wagon Alley off to Jackman's right. Tunney and Quill appeared bored and uninvolved as he prepared to read the riot act to the rancher, while every other Texan showed all too visibly tense and nervous. But of course it was the very fact that the gunmen were able to act that way with the stink of danger so thick in the very air, that hammered it home to Jackman that the pair were the real thing. Professionals.

Which set the professional tally at three on this street at this time. That pair and himself. And Jackman the town-tamer was never more determined that he would triumph no matter how McCord might react to what he had to say, or what the man might do.

He spoke simply and clearly.

'You will haul your freight and leave immediately, mister. All of you. You have one minute. Any Texan still on this street then will be arrested and charged with—'

'With interfering in your personal life, maybe, Marshal?' McCord cut in, his deep voice carrying. He gestured. 'But I'm sure you're all aware what this is really about, ladies and gentlemen. Your hired gun is on familiar terms with a lady I am courting, and has chosen to use his authority corruptly to ban me, a rival, from his town. Well, I doubt if these good people will tolerate that, Jackman, and you can be damned sure I won't. You are a low fake and a sham, Mister Gunner, and your gall and reputation don't impress me worth a spit.' He paused to lend his words weight.

'And of course, the same goes for my crew, proud and law-abiding Texans every one.' He swung abruptly and gave a hand signal. 'Boys, show this Yankee marshal

110

how we feel about his bogus, Kansas-hatched law, why don't you!'

Nobody even saw Jackman draw.

His gun was suddenly magically in his hand and he was pumping shots into the sky.

This was a technique he'd often used. If gunsmoke threatened, seize the initiative and be first to burn powder yourself. Mostly it threw the enemy, and it surely jolted the Pecos crew as they struggled to calm panicking horses, rolling their eyes at the man with the gun.

But Jackman was no longer interested in a bunch of shit-for-brains cowpushers. Was already pivoting to face the hitch rail as the only two men who'd not been spooked by his gunblasts reached deliberately for their Colts.

It was get-square time for Mac Tunney and Olan Quill and they grabbed gun handles and slipped into low crouches like the well-rehearsed double act they were.

But Jackman had a sixshooter in his fist already. Cocked. Aimed.

The gun bucked to drill two warning shots between the pair. Startled, shocked, they executed leaps in opposite directions. Clay's left-hand gun swept up and he shot Quill deliberately through the knee as the Texan made to fire. The gunman's scream was high-pitched and ululating like a woman's as he crashed to ground. Tunney stood silhouetted against the gloom of the alley-mouth, gun at firing-level but freezing now as Jackman swept his smoking muzzle up on him.

'Use it or drop it, Tunney!'

The gunman did not respond quickly enough and Jackman's finger was tightening on trigger, when he unaccountably froze. For a hanging moment neither man moved: the marshal caught leaning forward aggressively, gun outstretched before him; Mac Tunney reared back on his heels with his .45 angled somewhere in the direction of Jackman's boots, feral face drained of blood as his downed partner's moans of agony washed over him.

And Mace Street stared.

Why weren't the guns thundering?

Only Jackman knew. Only he could see, through failing eyes, the mouth of the alley, the water-barrels and the dim stir of movement there directly behind the fear-locked figure of his adversary.

Slowly Tunney worked the ice out of his limbs. His Colt rose steadily but still Jackman did not respond. Desperately Tunney wanted to shoot, but dare not go so far, not with the marshal crouched out there in the sunlight with a Colt in either hand, he didn't.

'Better dust if you ain't got the belly to fight, Jackman,' he ventured, still unsure if words might not bring a storm of lethal lead in response.

Jackman shuddered and straightened. Then his guns were sliding into leather and his back was to the gunman as he walked away. Yet such was the lingering impact of his total domination of the scene and the sheer force of his personality, that Tunney found it impossible to grasp the full import of what was happening, had no time or the presence of mind to do more than yell: 'Yellow belly!' and 'You are just another fake, Jackman!' before the town-tamer was gone down River

Street without a word, without once looking back.

'What's happening now?' demanded Klegg Sands from the depths of his deep leather chair in the town board's conference room.

'Take a look,' Brawn Carter grunted to a heavyweight with a well-oiled cowlick. Mostly the heavyweight tended bar at the Republic saloon up the block, but tonight found himself, along with the bar's three bouncers, handling a security detail for their employer and his close friend the mayor.

One thing was rock-solid certain. Neither Sands nor Carter wanted to display themselves in any lighted window until they had some idea just which way the wind was blowing on a night as fraught with uncertainty as any in Chisum's history.

Cowlick fingered the drapes back cautiously. Streetlights burned and false-fronts stood tall against a sea of stars. Two dogs, a slow moving bum and a tense-looking man on a bay horse clattering by were the only signs of life. Of course, had the man elected to open the window and stick his head out his field of vision would be greatly enhanced. Instead he allowed the drapes to fall back and tried to look reassuring as he turned to the staring room.

'Quiet as the grave.'

The words were barely out of his mouth when a single gunshot rolled down Mace Street.

Ten men, six board members and their protection, waited in slack-jawed silence for the hostile sound to be repeated, or perhaps to discover that it was actually the opening salvo by the barbarians from the South in what

113

might well prove to be the destruction of their town.

In the white-knuckle aftermath of the débâcle on Mace Street earlier, fear, imagination, guilt and dread were running rampant through the city upon the river. The board had gone to extreme lengths in order to recapture the town's authority over the enemy, had seemed to be winning every hand until exactly 4.27 p.m. when the wheels had come off their cart with a crash still faintly echoing in their ears.

Tall men wearing chaps and long spurs roamed empty streets on horses with burrs in their tails, taking experimental sixgun sightings on such targets as the town hall clock, the statue of the Civil War general imported from a boomtown which had died and had no further use for heroes; even the front doors of the courthouse.

Nobody had been hurt or killed, so far as was known here in the adjunct of the courthouse. This was the first gunshot heard since Mac Tunney exuberantly emptied his gun into the false-front of the Chisum City Food and Grain Store to mark the marshal's bewildering disappearance.

It was some time before Brawn Carter heaved himself out of his chair to break the silence.

'Just letting off steam,' he surmised, heading for the liquor cabinet. The gesture he made was a failed attempt at nonchalance. 'Cowboys are like that as we should know. High-spirited and cussed at times but no real harm in them deep down.'

'They are butchering, illiterate Secessionist scum!' countered Sands, red-faced with embarrassment at the naked fear he'd just displayed while waiting for the second shoe to drop.

'They're toying with us. McCord is out there some-where crowing and strutting like the Texan redneck he is, holding them back while we sweat, knowing he's got the whip hand and can take us any damn time he pleases now. So don't give me any of that simple coun-try boys having a good time horseshit, Carter. We're in deep trouble and anyone who says different is a blind fool.'

Carter gulped down his brandy and looked resentful. Mostly at such times this was as far as he went where Sands was concerned. For it was Sands's money that had set him up in the saloon, Sands's patronage and advice that saw him prosper, Sands the icon he was modelling himself upon.

Then it hit like a housebrick that they'd never been in a situation like this and Sands was responsible. And the walls of restraint and caution came down with a crash, the crash of Carter hurling his glass into the cold hearth.

'A fool?' he challenged, veins protruding from his forehead, head thrust forward on bull neck. 'Whose idea was it to hire Jackman in the first place? And whose brainstorm was it to use him to dump the posting ordi-nance on the Pecos herd as a way of chopping off any notion Clay might've had of taking up with the Fallon woman where he left off last year and maybe taking her back home with him?'

'How dare you!'

'I dare right enough, Mr Mayor! If this town goes under it's your doing. And if you're thinking of fore-closing on my loan, think again. Your ace has been cancelled, the sheriff's twice my man as he is yours, and if we get out of this mess you've walked us into alive there's going to be a new boss in this burg and his name will be Carter. You hear me, you pile of dung?'

The mayor was stunned. It was not enough that the enemy without was at the gates, but now the false allies within were rebelling, showing their true, treacherous colours and nailing them up.

Sands made to speak but Carter formed a fist the size of a bowling ball and shoved it silently within an inch of his nose. In the distance someone laughed loudly, a harsh braying sound in this unnatural quiet. It was not Harlen McCord. But had the cattleman known how swiftly and abysmally the fabric of the town was unravelling without his raising a finger, he would have had good reason to laugh long and hard. For none knew better than the major that Chisum's darkest hours were yet to come.

'Sorry,' Bowie told the new arrivals, speaking over the batwing doors. 'We're not doing business tonight, gentlemen.'

'Why the tarnation not, man?' one of the thirsty towners complained. 'If there was ever a night a man needed a drink it's tonight.'

'Sorry. Miss Carla's orders.'

'But the Republic's closed too,' said another. 'Only decent place that's servin' is the Yellow Dollar, and that's full of Texicans.'

'Likkerin'-up Texicans,' the third added ominously. 'Somethin's brewin', Bowie. Better let us in.'

'The Painted Lady is closed!'

The sound of Carla Fallon's stern voice saw the towners back up. On the rare occasions she used that tone, it paid a man to pay attention.

'OK, OK,' muttered the leader, turning to go. 'Looks like we either go below the Deadline or go drink with stinkin' herders. . . .'

'Hey, Joe,' Bowie called over the swinging doors. 'Anyone see any sign of the marshal yet?'

'Nary a sign,' came the reply as the group drifted off. And another voice added, 'If he's anywhere he'd be at the Yellow Dollar after what happened today, don't you figure. . . ?'

Bowie's jaws tightened as he turned back to the bar.

'It's hard to figure. A man like the marshal builds his life on courage, falters once and the yapping dogs can't wait to start. . . .'

The man paused as he saw Carla pour herself another at the bar. This was confusing. The marshal never backed away from a fight and the boss lady never drank. Until now, it seemed. Everything was turned upside down tonight. But when the back door banged open and Johnny came striding in, tall, confident and clean-limbed, Bowie began to feel at least a little reassured.

The boy had sure changed of late. They were both aware of it, he and Miss Carla.

'Just came from the Yellow Dollar,' Johnny reported, going to the bar. 'Know what they are doing? Standing round the piano singing Dixie and boosting Tunney around the room on their shoulders like he's done something special.' He grimaced. 'Damnation! It wasn't that important, what happened. And we all know Clay had his reasons—'

'Have you seen Clay?' his sister interrupted.

The boy sighed and leaned his back against the bar.

'Nary a sign. And I've been all over – the Clayton House, every bar – all over. Of course you can guess what those cow pushers are saying. Claim he turned yellow, that he's quit town with his tail between his legs!'

Johnny tugged his gun from leather and spun it on his finger.

'Clay never ran from anything or anybody in his life,' he said soberly. 'Something happened to him out there, something bad. And when he comes sashaying through those doors he'll tell us what it was. He'll tell the Johnny Rebs too. He's not through with them yet, take it from me.'

'Here,' Bowie said, pushing a shot-glass at the boy. 'Get that down you and relax, Johnny. We all need to relax.'

Carla studied her brother's profile as he pushed the liquor aside. She didn't speak. It seemed that all her life she had worried about Johnny. But not tonight, for some strange reason. From almost the moment Jackman disappeared in the middle of a showdown, it seemed that her brother had acquired something she could only think of as a kind of instant maturity. He'd always been level-headed and reliable, but now there was a sense of power and assurance that hadn't been there before.

This both impressed and frightened her at the same time. Yet she welcomed this change, for she herself was weak tonight, worried. Not about her brother, the Texans or Chisum. Nor even her own safety. She would go on fretting until Clay came striding through her doors and she knew he was safe.

She couldn't care less about what had happened. People might cheer Jackman when he triumphed with the guns, or turn on him if he failed. None of that meant a thing to her. All she wanted for him now was all she had ever wanted. That he be all right . . . that he might come to her again as he once had done in Broken Bit. . . .

If nothing else, this ugly day had made her realize what he truly meant to her, and always would.

The three turned towards the batwings as the sound of horses being ridden at full gallop rose rapidly, reached a drumming crescendo as they passed, faded towards River Street.

'This town is getting liquored-up,' Bowie grunted. 'When it's drunk enough, something will happen.' His dark eyes flicked at the woman. 'Time we were gone, Miss Carla.'

'Gone?' she said irritably, wiping the bar. 'We're not going anywhere.'

'Sure we are,' the man countered. 'You see, this thing is really all about you, Missy. The mayor enforced that posting order to keep McCord out town, because of you. The marshal served it on the Pecos mob for the same reason. But the Texan rancher was not about to show weak in your eyes and just knuckle under, so he saddled up and came to town – just because of you.'

'I resent your saying that, Bowie,' she snapped. 'I think it's most unfair to blame me for this . . . this madness.'

'It's none of it your fault,' he replied evenly. 'But

what I say is still so, meaning that sooner or later you're going to get dragged into all this, and with the marshal gone there's no saying just how far it will go.'

Her eyes flared.

'Clay has not gone. He wouldn't leave. . . .'

She broke off uncertainly. But Bowie pressed: 'Leave what, Miss Carla? The town or you?'

'Me, damn you, Bowie,' she flared back. She touched her breast. 'Clay would never leave me if he thought I was in danger.'

'So, you admit you could be in danger here?'

A deep breath saw Carla regain her normal calm. 'I'd like you to stack the chairs on the tables, thank you, Bowie. We won't be doing any more business tonight. And do be smart about it, will you.'

The 'breed just shrugged and went to work. He'd said his piece, but she was still the boss. He had everything stacked, and Carla and her brother had finished with the bar and galley by the time he heard a vehicle roll up outside, the sound of voices.

The three traded looks. Moments later Mac Tunney pushed the batwings apart and sauntered in followed by Harlen McCord and six gun-hung Texans.

CHAPTER 8

THE LONGEST NIGHT

The room was dark but he had no trouble finding bottle, glass or cigars. As he lit up utilizing his engraved pocket-flint – the one presented to him in appreciation by the grateful citizens of Jacknife – the tiny flame was reflected in the spectacles he wore.

He sighed as he dragged deep, raised his glass and leaned back in his chair by the window. It might be the worst night of his life but at least he could see with razor-edged clarity. But then the corners of his mouth tugged down as he reminded himself that what he could see was a sight he had seen too often before, not here in Chisum, but in other places such as Jackson, Arkansas and Middleville, Oklahoma Territory.

He could see bolted doors, barred windows, frightened people on the streets and the menace of hellions swaggering about as free as jaybirds, looking for trouble and certain to find it. He heard his name shouted with derision accompanied by mocking laughter, and he didn't even care. This was how far the iron marshal had slipped in the space of simply a few hours. His birth date was 6 November. A Scorpio. Carla had once given him an astrological birthday card during their six months together, and he still recalled the printed verse:

All the way up, or all the way down,
On middle ground, no Scorpio is found.

He'd scorned the piece of doggerel at the time. Now it seemed profound, even prophetic. The guns had certainly taken him all the way up; now, if he was not 'all the way down', nobody ever was.

A soft footfall beyond the door.

His right hand leapt to the Thuer on the small table as the door opened and light flooded the room. He didn't even get to cock the piece. With spectacles, he had close to 20-20 vision. There was no mistaking Madam's blousy figure for some low-life herder eager to die.

The door closed behind her and he welcomed the darkness again. Attar of roses wafted over him as he returned his attention to the street, the Thuer still in hand. The sofa creaked behind him.

'You need anything?'

'Thank you, Madam, I have all I need.'

'Except good sense.'

'Pardon?'

'How long do you intend beating yourself to death for something that wasn't your fault?'

'I abrogated my duty. If that isn't my fault, whose is it?'

'I know what happened on the street, Marshal.'

He dragged on his cheroot, the crimson glow tinting his features as sharp and clear-cut as an etching. 'You were good enough to offer me sanctuary here where nobody would ever expect to find such an exemplarily moral man as myself, Madam, and I'm in your debt. But if you're aiming to take advantage of this situation to lecture me, or probe the town-tamer's troubled mind, you're wasting your time.'

Madam's perfumed sigh sounded.

'Don't you ever ease up?' she complained, getting to her feet. 'You're supposed to be relaxing here, but you sound just the way you do when you're lambasting those losers in the show-up room nights. OK, OK,' she added as he stirred, 'I'm leaving you to your self-pity . . . only hope you'll be happy together.' The door opened a crack. 'But I still know what happened—'

'Close it after you, lady.'

Instead, the door opened fully to reveal Bald George leaning on his cane standing in the hallway. The madam's man who could be her husband, handyman, pimp or procurer, gave him his wide, easy grin. But Jackman's face remained stone.

'What the hell is he doing here?' he demanded. 'Why don't you hang a banner from the balcony with He's Here! painted on it?'

'I'm posting George outside your door to make sure nobody gets up here.' The woman sniffed. 'And for your information, Marshal, he's the most reliable and trustworthy man you know.' The door began to close. 'George knows what happened too, but of course you don't want to talk about anything that might help you—'

'Goodnight!' Clay snapped.

He was left alone again in the darkness, the welcoming embracing darkness. Alone in the attic of a brothel in the shaking heart of a town teetering on the edge. He couldn't think of a better time or place for a man like him just to sit and plan out his future.

He laughed aloud at that as he refilled his glass from the brown bottle. He was a man of the gun with failing eyesight who'd seized upon a distraction as an excuse not to gun a man down, thereby holding himself up as a failure before the eyes of this town and ultimately the whole West.

What future was there for a two-gun town-tamer once he'd turned belly-up in a gunfight?

Slowly, deliberately, Mac Tunney extended his index finger to slide the empty shot-glass an inch closer to Johnny Fallon across the mahogany bar. The Texan's eyes glittered brightly and his smirk seemed have become permanent since his triumph on Mace Street.

'Whiskey,' he whispered for the third time. 'Pronto.' He paused, then had to add: 'Boy.'

'Bar's closed.'

Johnny tried to keep his voice even but didn't succeed. It was not fear that was shaking him but anger. Of all the Texans in town, this was the one he hated hardest. The Texas gun had knocked Clay from his pedestal before the eyes of the whole town. Johnny wanted an excuse to draw his gun and empty it into that lean, black-shirted chest. But he was no killer. He felt he had changed beyond belief in the space of a few short hours today, was still coming to terms with that. But he knew he'd not changed into a cold-blooded killer.

'Fill it or so help me I swear I'll put five miles of daylight through you, sister's boy!'

'You wouldn't have the balls to shoot a fly off a steak!' Johnny shot back before he caught himself. He shrugged, folded his arms, stared at the darkened ceiling.

Tunney just smiled malevolently.

'You're all het up, ain't you, snotnose?' he said softly. 'And why not, eh? Seems everyone in this dump knows you think the sun shines out of Jackman, and now with him turning pure yeller that way, you're back to being the nothing you were last year when he wasn't here, and what you're gonna be all over again now he's all washed up.'

'Clay will never be washed up,' Johnny Fallon said quietly. 'Something happened on the street today—'

'Sure did, and everyone seen it. They call it going to water.'

'You'd better stopper up that jaw of yours, Texan.'

'Or what, sister's boy?'

'Easy!' interjected Bowie, coming along the bar. He nodded at the couple seated at the table midway across the room. 'Seems to me your boss man is looking a little edgy over yonder, Texan. He mightn't appreciate your starting up something over here for no good reason.'

Tunney's sneer faded as he shot a look over his shoulder. He saw it was true. The boss, Harlen McCord, who'd arrived at the Painted Lady in such high spirits, now looked tight and pale around the jawline, his back ramrod-straight and shoulders hunched in tension.

The Texas gunman began rolling a Durham. Tunney

wanted to rip and tear tonight. Felt the need to consol-idate his elevated status achieved through Quill's wounding and the marshal's astonishing capitulation. The fast gun had a lot to prove in the wake of the humiliation of Jackman's visit to the herd, had many a score to settle with all the Texan-hating towners infest-ing this man's lousy town.

And there was more than that riding him tonight. He considered – when it came right down to cases – that the boss man was demeaning himself, coming cap in hand here to the Painted Lady, shaved, bathed, togged out in his best and stinking of lavender-water in the hope of getting to play kissy-face with Jackman's whore.

To Tunney's way of thinking, McCord simply didn't seem to realize they'd taken on a major battle here, that it was far from won. Apart from that, he'd like to remind McCord that in his position, he didn't have to ask, he could simply take.

He turned back to the silent Johnny.

'You might as well know you're on my list, junior!' he hissed. 'That dust-up on the street. Remember? You smashed up some good pards of mine . . . yeah, I know all about that. There's that and the fact that they tell me you and that yellow-gutted marshal are said to be real good pards. Just so soon as the boss stops playing Romeo and remembers what we owe this crummy dump, the hopples will be off and it'll be get-square time. Look for me then, boy, for Mac Tunney will sure come looking for you.'

'Go fry!' Johnny retorted. And it ended there when the gunman turned his back to make his lithe-hipped way towards the rear to join his fellow Texans killing time playing the roulette wheel.

Bowie patted Johnny's shoulder to calm him down. It seemed to work. The two then leaned against the bar watching Carla and McCord, studying their faces and looking for indicators as to how the meeting was going.

To the naked eye, it appeared as though it was going badly for the Texan, and that impression was dead on target.

The rancher had looked smart upon his arrival here. An hour at the barber shop followed by a good soak in the hot tubs at the Clayton House topped up by a change to fresh rig had brought the cattle king from the Pecos to the Painted Lady looking exactly the way he was feeling, like a man on top of the world.

Not any longer.

The purpose of his visit was to restate his case as the serious suitor he'd imagined himself to be when he'd visited the previous year. He was quite prepared to set aside today's dramatic confrontation, despite the significance it held for everyone in Chisum – Kansan and Texan alike. He was now inviting Carla Fallon to join him up in Dodge City after he'd delivered the herd in order that they might get to have a fine time, cement their relationship. McCord intimated he was not prepared to rule out the very real possibility of his making a formal proposal, providing, of course, that she still regarded herself as a free agent who might find such a proposition both feasible and agreeable.

The cattle king was skilled at outlining deals and propositions.

He had been doing so successfully all his life. But within the space of half a minute the mistress of the

Painted Lady, finding herself placed in a position where straight talking was called for, had revealed that her gentleman caller from the Pecos didn't have a patent on straight talk.

She rejected his proposition out of hand. Insisted she had never regarded the rancher in any light other than that of a respected friend. And when McCord paled and demanded to know if there was someone else, specifically if that someone could be Clay Jackman, Carla stared him straight in the eye and said: 'Yes, I love Clay although he doesn't love me.'

Encouraged by that admission, he'd spent twenty minutes attempting to talk her round without success.

Suddenly she rose.

'I really am sorry. Now, if there is nothing else, Harlen. . . ?'

'That's it?' he gasped, getting up. 'I . . . I come here ready to offer you the world and you brush me off like some nobody. Just like that. You're admitting you'd prefer to moon over a cheap guntoter gone bad than Harlen McCord?'

Carla lifted her chin.

'You're forcing me to say this, but Clay Jackman is ten times the man you'll ever be.'

There was irony in the fact that in his immediate reaction to this blow to his vanity, the Texan went a long way towards affirming the accuracy of her insult.

He lashed back as only someone less than a gentleman would. 'By Taos you'll regret this, woman. You and your guntoting gigolo and this whole stinking mare's nest of a Jayhawker pest-hole you operate. Every citizen here is guilty of supporting Sands in importing your gunman to humiliate and denigrate me and my people, and by God every citizen will regret it.'

He whirled away, his face coloured hectically, the personification of a big man burning with Texas pride and Texas wrath.

'Tunney, all of you!' he shouted, stamping for the doors. 'We're leaving, which as sure as shooting isn't saying we won't be back!'

As his men hurried after the powerful figure, Mac Tunney paused to turn his hat in slim brown hands and smiled icily round the room.

'Well, you have surely gone and done it now, *amigos.*' His words dripped with malice. 'I doubt if the boss has been so mad since he took on you Bluecoat white trash at Shiloh schoolhouse.' He fitted his hat to his head and flicked a mocking salute at Carla. 'Pity, you'd have made a fine-looking mistress of Pecos Ranch, lady. Now I guess you'll have to count yourself lucky if you even get to make old bones.' He headed out, looking back over his shoulder. 'And I reckon that goes double for junior.'

It grew quiet in the Painted Lady Saloon.

The scream ripped through the night and caused Sands's smooth grey hair to stand on end.

'What in God's name was that?' he whispered.

'Sounded like a woman,' Carter replied in a voice that sounded as though his fat mouth was stuffed with cotton wool. 'Might have come from the Yellow Dollar, and it sure didn't sound good.'

The two men stared at one another. They stood in the darkened doorway of the general store where they'd taken cover when a party of five herders riding at the gallop tore the full length of Mace Street, turned at the fire station, then thundered back to dismount noisily and drunkenly at the Yellow Dollar.

Even more noticeably than before, Chisum was locking down, drawing the drapes and battening the hatches as the very air seemed to throb with something even more menacing and ominous.

Klegg Sands alone knew how desperately he needed to go completely to ground, get the hell out of here and surround himself with security and secrecy until the last Texan was gone and he might resume his authority and status again.

The weakness in his bowels and the slow thudding of his heart told him what he had always suspected: Chisum's Mr Big was yellow clear through. Corrupt and cowardly.

Texans now owned the town and Sands had brought it all about by abusing his position of authority in hiring the Gunner to go deal with his perceived rival.

If he survived, Sands might look back and see events in a romantic light; his risking so much and daring so recklessly for a woman he believed he just had to have.

The shock of learning of Jackman's and Carla Fallon's past relationship had hit hard, yet faded into insignificance alongside the marshal's collapse today. And in that dragging minute of silence following the awful shriek from the Yellow Dollar, nothing signified for the mayor so much as his personal safety.

Nobody knew that the buggy and pair which left the town quietly by River Street some ten minutes later contained their mayor and owner of the Republic.

The first rats had deserted the sinking ship. But they would not be the last.

CHAPTER 9

BURNING BRIGHT

It was below the Deadline, where trouble usually originated, where the potent fuse of Texas hostility first sputtered then flared into ugly full life.

A Deadline woman had been stabbed and killed up at the Yellow Dollar, whether intentionally or accidentally was not clear. All that was certain was that a cowboy was responsible. Word of the tragedy was yet to spread beyond the Deadline, yet quickly found its way to the rough bar where scores of Cimarron City's largely Mexican and black unemployed assembled together both for security and reassurance as the danger barometer continued to plummet.

The effect of the grim news was exactly as if somebody had thrown a switch.

In an instant the temper of the crowd was ignited and an unlucky Texan drinker was set upon by raging drunks and screaming women. The blurred mirror in back of the plank bar went down with a crash, and a wild Rebel yell resounded outside.

Texans in the street!

Suddenly guns were storming and a stampede of terror erupted as figures went down bloodily and the coughing snarl of sixguns sounded like big animals roaring at one another in the misting night.

A woman in a nightgown ducked beneath a hitch rail and fled into an alley. Two riders rode after her, yipping and howling, one swinging a lariat. Her cries became screams of terror.

Chisum's nightmare had begun.

Locked away from it all in an upstairs room of a bordello, sipping blended bourbon and feeling remote from the roar and rumble of a town coming apart, might have appeared an unlikely place for a man like Clay Jackman to get his thoughts and emotions straightened out.

Yet something seemed to be working as he extracted a stogie from an inside pocket of his dark coat and cracked a vesta into life on a thumbnail.

He realized it might have been as long as twenty years since Jackman the marshal had taken a long hard look at Jackman the man in the harsh light of changing realities.

He blinked. He blinked much more often than he'd done in the old days. But suspect eyesight didn't prevent him looking back with twenty-twenty vision.

Two decades earlier, as a novice law enforcer still uncertain of his niche, the marshal had made an objective self-survey and discovered and defined exactly who and what he was, what he wished to be.

Suddenly everything had been plain.

He had no taste for commerce, cattle, clerking, opening up new lands, challenging the wilderness, going into banking, mining or sponging off rich women.

His talents were limited to gunspeed and a certain cool nerve which pointed him towards the single arena in which such skills might be both exercised and honoured, namely the law.

That he'd been both successful and lucky in his choice of career, there was no doubt. And perhaps he would not even be questioning it now, twenty years on, but for failing health. Yet in this dangerous night he was able to see clearly that, even if it hadn't been the eyes, something else would be warning him to get off the streetcar now.

Get off before it crashed and he became just another dead 'legend' like so many others.

Now suddenly he was off it.

Not the way he might have wanted to step down, perhaps. But beggars could not be choosers. Too bad he must now leave both Chisum and Carla, but that was the way the dice had rolled. There could be nothing for a town-tamer with feet of clay here. A lawman's professional life was over the moment he showed weakness before the enemy. . . .

The stairway creaked, bringing him back to the reality of the here and now.

Seated with the cocked Thuer in his fist and again growing aware of the externals which had been blotted out by his introspection, he smelt smoke and cordite, dust and horses. The rumble of hoofbeats and sporadic gunshots were punctuated by shouting and singing and there was the stridently incongruous racket of an open-topped piano being played at breakneck tempo some-place close by.

His town was drinking, fear-ridden and slowly coming apart at the seams and there was nothing he could do about it. A town-tamer might be afforded many opportunities to display his courage but could only count on one shot at exhibiting his cowardice.

'I'm fixed all right for everything, Madam,' he said, anticipating his visitor as she appeared silhouetted in the doorway.

'What about information?' Madam retorted. 'How are you fixed for that commodity?'

'If you have information you should tell someone who's interested.' He took a pull of his bottle but the liquor taste was starting to sour. Light glinted from his spectacles as he angled his head to glance past the woman at her man. 'You've done a fine job steering everyone away from here, George. Keep it up.'

'George's got something to tell you, Marshal,' the woman said.

'Let me guess. Bad news?'

'I seen it,' said George, taking Madam's place in the doorway as she entered the room. His bald head gleamed as he gestured. 'They're calling you for every-thing that's low out on the streets, Mr Jackman, but I seen what happened.'

'Oh yes?' Jackman hardly cared. What had taken place on the street seemed of little consequence now. He was already a vastly different man from the one who'd cut one gunslinger down and had the other at his mercy when the wheels came off.

'I was heading for the big showdown when I heard the shot. I started hustling down Wagon Lane when I seen that Tunney feller come lunging sideways on to Mace, and you were there with smoke swirlin' all around you and your sixgun aimed square at him – and of course, at them kids.'

'The Jackson boys from the Deadline,' Madam interjected. 'Little Rick and Micky. He seen them. Go on, George.'

Baldy George shrugged. and spread his hands. They were white and uncalloused. He was an old pimp.

'Yeah . . . plain as paint it was to me what happened at that point, Mr Marshal. You seen straight off that if you cut loose at that guntipper you could have easy killed them little squirts in the alley direct in back of him. So you quit. Now ain't that the simple truth?'

It was. The very simple truth. But what had befallen him out on that street had been coming for at least eighteen months now. Two years earlier, had he found himself caught up in that exact situation, he would have cut loose and killed his man as neat as dotting an i with no risk of collateral damage. But the present day Clay Jackson, sitting here with his bottle and with his spectacles in his pocket, had realized that if one of his bullets had missed their intended target he could have easily killed a child in the alley-mouth in the background.

Sometimes it seemed to him he'd built a whole career out of risk-taking, but he wouldn't go to face his Maker with something like that on his conscience.

In any case, now that he was done and every man and his brother thought the worst of him, it was almost a relief. It would be a complete relief if only he could fully switch off his nagging feeling of responsibility.

So he took another pull on the bottle and half-grinned at the irony in the fact that, half-liquored though he was, he sensed he was seeing almost as well as ever. Yet the question of whether he'd had just reason to quit and thereby turn the town over to the Texans, didn't signify all that much now. He saw the whole incident as something meant to happen to free him from of the locked-in life of twenty years before some hellion's bullet freed him for ever.

'Are those kids OK now?' he enquired.

'Sure . . . little squirts. I sent them off with a boot in the backside and they called me a baldy old bastard. . . .' George broke off, head cocked sharply. 'Somethin' going on downstairs,' he muttered and headed for the stairs, leaving Madam and marshal alone.

'I knew it all along,' the woman said firmly. 'You're no coward no matter what they might be saying.'

His shrug was eloquent and Madam read it like clear print.

'You've really handed in your resignation, haven't you?' she asked eagerly. She tapped her forehead. 'Up here, I mean. You're just not worrying about whatever the Sam Hill they are saying or doing any more. But this is wonderful, you know, Marshal. From the first moment I clapped eyes on you I said, "Florence, this man's too good to be risking his life shooting it out with bums every day of the week." And then when I heard about you and that lovely Miss Fallon—'

'Don't get carried away,' he said, rising and stretching. 'Miss Fallon's got her life here and I've got to find mine, wherever it might be. . . .'

137

She touched his arm.

'You'll find it easy enough if you're truly ready to give the old life away,' she insisted. 'Look at my George. Ten years back he was the wagon-racing rodeo champ of the South-west; nobody could touch him. Then a wagon rolled over his legs and his rodeoing days were over. But look at him now, no excitement or danger, but he's got me and I've got him . . . and he's alive. You can make it if you believe you can.'

She was saying what Jackman wanted to hear even if he didn't quite believe it yet.

He stiffened as a storm of gunshots erupted from somewhere below the Deadline. But after a moment he simply shook his head and reached for his hat. Cold turkey was the only way to cut it. Maybe he might risk stopping by at the Lady for just a moment, but after that he would be gone. Riding. Alone, of course. That was the only way for him, and better for Carla.

He went out on the landing with Madam when George's bald dome appeared in the muted lamplight below, resembling the egg of some giant bird. The man looked up with a face knotted with concern.

'It's that young feller, Mr Marshal,' he called. 'Johnny from the Painted Lady. He just horned in on some kind of dust-up 'twixt a couple of herders and a bunch of the boys in the alley. He pistol-whipped 'em good like you wouldn't believe. But now they've whistled up some pards and are after him scone-hot. I got to have a few words with him afore the bunch showed. But he's sore as a boil. Said he was fed up to the back teeth of all they are saying against you, and mad about what them hell-riders are doin' to the town. Claims there's people been killed and raped. Matter of fact Johnny said he was on his way to draw out McCord's second "fang". He sure sounded like he meant it.'

Gazing down as fear-filled faces emerged to stare up at him, Jackman felt a chill. He was reluctant to comment, but found it impossible not to.

'Fang?' He sounded almost irritated. 'What did he mean by that?'

'He reckons Tunney and Quill are the teeth of that Pecos herd. So I guess with Quill out of action he meant he's going after Tunney, Mr Marshal.'

Jackman stared at Madam's worn, painted face.

'Don't let them sucker you back in, Jackman,' she pleaded. 'You've made your break and you simply don't want to do it any more. That Fallon boy might be as gutsy and high-minded as they come, but he's still only a cocky boy who talks too much. If he lands in something he can't handle then it's no longer any concern of yours. Right now, standin' here, you're out of that town-tamin' business – and not afore time either if them grey streaks over your ears is anything to go by. . . .'

There was more but he didn't hear. And despite his almost detached manner as he moved the woman to one side and started down the steep stairs, the bitter taste was rising in his throat and corded muscles along his jawline jumped and writhed like steel wire beneath the taut skin.

It was but twenty steps down to ground-level but it might have been the longest journey of his life for a man who had been walking the streets, staircases and darkened alleyways of the West for twenty years.

He supposed now he'd realized all along that he could not simply just walk away.

He might feel like a reformed alcoholic being held down to have liquor forced down his throat, yet there was no alternative. There never was.

He almost envied Bald George as he stepped past the oldster and crossed the parlour's carpeted floor. The surging roar of a town out of control reached his ears again but nothing would slow his steps.

It could have been Carla, and the dread of what might befall her later as the possible perceived real cause of the Sands-McCord friction, that was driving him outside. But more likely it was simply the ground-in habit of a lifetime never to leave any job unfinished, that had clicked in, and was now driving him down the dark pathway towards the sinister-seeming lights.

Could have been either or both, yet wasn't.

It was simply the kid.

He knew what Johnny would be feeling and how he was thinking right now. For Jackman had been Johnny Fallon twenty years ago.

He stepped out into the street, Spartacus fed to the lions.

'Sweet Judas, who kicked the shit can over?' mouthed the battered drunk as the tall figure loomed up through smoke and sifting dust on the courthouse corner. 'Lookit, boys, it's our fire-breathing dragon of a town-tamer, as I live and breathe. And here was I believin' I'd been left to fend for myself while stinkin' Texicans busted me up and stove in my ribs!' He coughed crimson and fumbled for the gun protruding

140

from the waistband of his chinos. 'You yeller bastard, Jackman, I'm gonna—'

The towner's intentions were only too plain. But his words was cut short when Jackman booted his feet from under him, then kicked him in the jaw with a sound like an axe biting wet wood. The man gasped and passed out leaving the marshal facing his companions, his face invisible in the black shadow of his hat.

The men cringed back, exactly as he expected. He had no time for diversions, for he suspected that Johnny had likely gone looking to quell the worsening trouble at the Yellow Dollar.

Striding on more swiftly now, he barely recognized the town he'd taken over and pacified. While he'd been confronting his demons tonight, vengeful Texans were venting their wrath on a town that now resembled a war zone.

He thought of Hickok the night he had shut down Trail Street, Abilene, of Wyatt Earp confronting the Clantons in Tombstone. They had survived their moments of truth, yet he doubted their situations had been this grim. Neither of those practitioners of his bloody craft had had to overcome showing yellow in the face of the enemy.

Even though he was ready to put his life on the line for a friend, he knew his heart was no longer in the game.

This made a huge difference, yet he was reassured by two things. He felt as committed and confident as ever, hurrying through this dust-red and gunsmoke-grey miasma which seemed to fill Mace Street from false-front to false-front. But best of all, the wire-framed spectacles he wore now ensured he could see clearly. And he wondered why he'd allowed his foolish gunfighter's vanity to dictate that it was more important that he look the part than worry about his own safety.

He adjusted his spectacles.

Someone had deemed the play must go on – right to the final curtain.

A fire-wagon, drawn by four snorting horses and manned by towners in red hats and yellow suspenders hanging on to the handrail, went storming by in the direction of Aimes Street, where flames and smoke roiled into the sky.

He lifted his pace to a jogging run. A hundred yards on, when he paused to glance at a towner slumped on a bench, clutching a bullet-bloodied shoulder, a herder came loping up out of an alley, spotted him and kicked his horse closer.

'Reckoned it was you, lawdog!' The rider was long, unwashed and slack of jaw. 'B'God, wonderman, you should have stayed beneath that rock you crawled under, for I'm surely gonna show you what happens to chicken-guts lawdogs in big old eyeglasses when the real men come to Kansas – yessiree!'

The drunken herder was fumbling for his side-arm. Jackman whipped out the Thuer, lunged forward and swung it with all his might. The savage blow smashed the Texan's forearm above the wrist and he screamed like a woman as the startled horse carried him across the street and out of sight.

Jackman continued on, thrusting the heavy sixshooter back into leather and flexing his fingers.

He grimaced in the eerie light of a burning barn and

saw himself as though from a distance; the Gunner gearing up to take on a town running wild and out of control. Just one more time.

Again he halted.

Up ahead, emerging from the thick smoky air, moving figures. A silent, advancing group of towners appeared like ghosts. At their head came four men, shoulder to shoulder, toting a door on which lay the body of a woman dressed like a percenter. In the distorting streetlight, the woman seemed to float four feet above the darkened plankwalk. The total silence that marked the advance of the party, with only the brush of boot-leather against board to be heard, and the shimmering effect of lamplight on the motionless figure in gold and white, caused the hairs on the back of Jackman's neck to rise.

'What happened?' he called, but they didn't seem to see or hear. And only now, sluggishly at the start but rapidly rising, did he feel the outrage and the anger kick in, sending the lethal iciness flowing down his long arms into his hands, his fingertips.

Murdering bastards!

He was no longer gearing himself up against his will as he went on now. What he'd seen was a vivid reminder of what he had been, what he might be one more time. Something raw and unquenchable was rising from the boards beneath his boots, from the very earth itself. Smokes and colours roiled overhead and the whole night seemed to pulsate and drum in his ears. A drunk came lunging towards him and Jackman whipped up the gun and smashed him clear off the walk to land on his head with a sickening thud. His eyes cut every which way searching for a tall kid with a gun. Someone shouted his name and a rifleman bobbed up from behind a false-front atop the stage depot. The moment the figure threw the rifle to his shoulder Jackman slipped low and fanned three bullets from his gun. The figure howled and fell, smashing its way through a board awning before slamming into the street, narrowly missing a horseman who'd paused to stare across at the lawman.

His next bullet shaved the rider's jaw and caused him to set spurs and take off, bawling: 'It's Jackman! The yeller-guts tin-star is back, and he just kilt Duggan!'

The rider was approaching the corner of the feed and grain barn when he whipped out a Colt and touched off a wild shot back in Jackman's direction.

Without pausing in his stride the town-tamer triggered without apparent aim and the rider nose-dived to earth with a sudden third eye in his forehead.

The reverberations of that shot distorted Jackman's hearing momentarily, and as it faded he realized he could hear a storm of shooting from some distance further along. It seemed to come from the direction of the Yellow Dollar where the hitch rail was lined with frightened horses sporting Texan brands.

He began to run, praying he was not too late.

CHAPTER 10

TEXANS IN TOWN

After just one drink at the dive on the corner, Johnny Fallon hurried on, keeping close to the shadowy buildings. When he saw the lights of the Yellow Dollar his face tightened and he paused, pressing his back flat against the wall of the bank. Riders came hell for leather down the centre of the street and he didn't move until they swept by. He heard their voices, twanging and alien-sounding in this nerve-tearing night. Texans.

Momentarily the street lay empty.

He darted forward, very conscious of the .45 riding his hip. His lips were dry and he gasped when he stumbled over someone lying in the gloom. He grabbed out his gun but it was only a drunk, slobbering and moaning. He didn't even know whether he was a towner or a Texan. It didn't matter. All that mattered was that it was not Tunney.

Mac Tunney.

He rolled the name round his mouth and his heart began to trot.

In the hours since Clay had vanished off the streets and chaos overtook his town, Johnny Fallon had undergone a cosmic change.

For years he'd simply dabbled at the law he loved, played with it, at times had linked himself with it, as at the jailhouse. Never totally sure where he was headed, always conscious of his sister's attitudes, yet always feeling that he'd been holding back in his life.

Until today.

The moment Clay disappeared and the Texans began to howl, he realized this was the day he would either follow his star or skulk away and never dream of walking in the footsteps of Clay and the other great town-tamers again.

He'd made his decision with ridiculous ease, was now no longer a boy but a man committed to everything he'd always believed in and dedicated to fighting for it.

Clear-headed, cool and intensely alert, he was convinced his thinking had to be right. He knew he couldn't prevail against a swarm of drunken Texans single-handed. Didn't believe he would have to. He'd observed the way the herders reacted when Quill had gone down under Jackman's gun. They had been gripped by sudden panic and uncertainty that had threatened to rout them, until Tunney snatched up the reins again to be supported eventually by McCord and the full force of the cattleman at his command.

And he thought: just two men!

He wasn't contemplating tackling a score of Texas cow-punchers fired up on whiskey and Lone Star pride. He saw the enemy as a two-headed hydra. McCord and his right bower, Mac Tunney. If he could destroy those

146

heads, then the cowhand 'body' of the hydra might well collapse and Chisum could yet be saved.

Sounded simple when you said it fast. Yet even when panic and doubt tried to raise their heads, his resolve remained rock-solid.

'Right will triumph!' he panted aloud. If Clay had said those words to him once over the years, he'd done so a score of times. It was a mantra he lived by. If it worked for him, why not for Johnny Fallon?

Everything hinged on Tunney, he reaffirmed. That gunner was the enemy's right bower and rallying point in this final bloody game which was devouring his town, threatening the only people who really mattered to him, his sister and Clay. Cut off a rattler's head and it would surely die. Wasn't that what folks said?

He slowed warily as he reached a corner of the Yellow Dollar, then darted down an alleyway. He made fast time and rounded behind the high unpainted building to approach the back gallery at the trot. Two yellow lanterns burned dully and several doors stood open, from which poured the sounds of riotous music and voices. Texan music and Texan nasal twangs. The devil was in the driving-seat in there.

Johnny walked to the door of one of the rooms, not wishing to meet some unwashed herder lurching down a passageway to relieve himself at the two-holer in back should he take that route. He eased the door fully open and stepped inside. For a moment he blinked in the semi-darkness. The only light came from a thick candle burning before the framed picture of a haloed saint. By its dim glow a naked man and woman were making love with such enthusiasm that they were unaware of the intruder until Johnny's gun butt thudded against the man's head. He grunted once and crashed to the floor on his back. A Texan, and an unconscious one now.

The girl was filling her lungs to scream when he shoved the muzzle of his gun between her breasts. 'Tunney, Vicky. Is he out there?'

'Y-yes, but what are you doing here, Johnny?'

'Whereabouts . . . exactly?' He needed to know. Every detail was vital. Frightened whispered words tumbled from the girl's red wound of a mouth. 'The back bar!' Then she fell silent, eyes huge. Touching a warning finger to his lips he swung away and padded down the passageway.

He paused once just long enough to lick his lips and suck in a huge breath.

His heart hammered hard, yet there seemed to be a centre of calm deep in his belly. He knew he was no gun honcho, that the odds against his accounting for this gunpacker had to be slim, and before tonight that understanding would have deterred him.

But not tonight.

For in his steely mind-set of the moment, he knew he was here simply to kill Tunney, not shoot it out with the man by any set of foolish rules.

He came swiftly into the crowded room, eyes scanning for his man at the short back bar. He sighted him almost instantly. The gunman was hatless, smirking and sun-bronzed beneath a bright light as he stood with one long arm around a woman's waist, nodding his head at something another Pecos hand was saying.

'This is for the marshal and for Chisum, Tunney!'

148

His shout cut through the bar sounds like a gunshot, and alarm turned to panic when they saw him standing there with a naked .45 in his fist, not genial Johnny Fallon, Carla's kid brother, but a steely-eyed man with lamplight glinting off the big gun in his fist.

Men and women went diving for the floorboards in mindless panic as the Texan guntipper launched into his deadly draw.

Johnny's gun belched flame and the woman along-side Tunney screamed and clutched her shoulder as she slumped back against the bar.

His next shot drilled only smoky air where the fast-footed gunman had been standing seconds before, and destroyed a bottle of sourmash on the shelves.

Tunney was down on one knee, fanning a gun hammer, the compounding crash of the shots within the confined space painful to the eardrums.

A lance of hot pain raked Johnny's ribcage but he was still standing, still felt strangely calm as he came lunging forward with his sixgun bucking back against the crotch of his hand as it emptied its lethal load.

And suddenly Tunney slumped against the bloodied bar with his long Texan jaw sagging agape, wild staring eyes already glazing over.

The guntipper was dead!

Scrabbling for fresh slugs in his jacket pocket, Johnny refused to take his eyes from that suspended figure, certain this was some slick Texan trick to throw him off guard. Then a gun bellowed, a bullet droned close and he dived behind a bench laden with empties and finally closed his hand over the bullets. Loading up fast, he kept low. The racket was terrifying, deafening, yet all he could think of was that he wasn't scared. He wasn't scared!

A swift stutter of steps sounded crossing the saloon porch and heads jerked in that direction. The batwings burst open and Olan Quill, limping, strapped-up and gaunt-faced came lunging into the sickly glow of the lights with men toting guns in back of him.

Squinting through a chink in the bar, Johnny felt a chill. He'd counted Quill out of the game!

The gunman paused as Texan voices shouted a warning. At that moment Mac Tunney's body finally slipped from where it had caught against the bar and landed with a sodden thud on the floor. Tunney fell face down in a pool of light and every eye saw the gaping red-lipped wounds where Fallon's bullets had exploded out his back.

A dizzy blonde tried to scream but her throat was too tight.

But her strangled sounds seemed to unlock the frozen tableau comprising crouched new arrivals, figures lurking behind upturned tables, the couple peering down from the upstairs landing.

And suddenly what was being shouted at him registered with Quill, who moved with the agility of a healthy man to gain the cover of a sturdy roof-support in the centre of the room.

In the sucked-out silence uncertainty prevailed for a moment. Johnny drew in his breath and tried to assess the odds. Maybe a dozen angry cowpokes, he calculated. Plus Quill. If he had Hickok on one side of him and Clay on the other, these odds would still be too steep.

Quill brandished his silver-plated cutter and howled like a dog-wolf.

'Let's not kill this son of a bitch straight out, boys!' he roared! 'He's just killed the best Texican what ever drew breath, and what we'll do to him will teach every Union scumsucker in this stinking territory that it was the South what lost their stinking war, not almighty Texas!'

Then he slewed towards the row of upturned tables sheltering a pale-faced Harlen McCord and his gun escorts, trapped there by Fallon's one-man invasion.

'I warned you that you were taking it too easy on the dirty Yankees, boss man!' he shouted at the big man crouched behind the biggest table. 'This snotnose what done for Tunney could have killed me, and you would have been next. You can't trust one of them, so I say let's get serious and do this job right . . . finish it here and now – all of it . . . take out every mother's son who's aginst us, startin' with him.'

With these words the gunslinger pumped a roaring volley of hot lead into the bar front that had Johnny hugging floorboards with cold sweat stinging his eyes.

Men coughed and choked from the cordite fumes as they attempted to build up to a roar of support for Quill, until the sound swiftly cut off as though a switch had been thrown. Quill hipped around, searching for the cause. He didn't see it at first, yet could certainly feel that something had gone awry with the room and its atmosphere. For everybody should be focused on him, whereas many were now twisting and turning to gaze upwards. As voices began to fade he felt a chill. What was it that they could see but he could not?

Resolution gripped him. He would command the floor or die trying! He took one purposeful lunge forward but froze as movement caught the corner of his eye.

He whirled with a gasp.

He found himself staring upwards at a tall figure all in brown and sporting eyeglasses who'd appeared upon the upper landing and now stood in plain view almost directly beneath a smoking oil lamp suspended from the invisible high ceiling.

'Is Johnny dead?'

Jackman's voice carried to every corner. And something about his very stance, the light glinting off steel-rimmed spectacles and his total motionlessness beneath that smoke-wreathed chandelier held them in momentary suspended animation. Texan, towner, all of them.

The man who had cowed the mob once before that day was doing so again.

'He's dead and so are you!' Quill screamed in raging fury, and whipped up his Peacemaker in a blue blur. But Jackman's hands filled with guns swifter than any eye could follow, and skilled fingers depressed the curved steel of the triggers.

He didn't miss.

His brutal volley slaughtered Quill in a swirling spray of crimson that spattered a far wall as he went down as though smitten by the hand of God. Smoothly Clay pivoted from the hips to drill a bullet through the heart of a bulky wrangler coming out of his bucket-chair with a huge knife balancing on the tips of spatulate fingers, ready to throw.

152

The Texan fell backwards and McCord sprang erect, bellowing to his men to stand like Texans and deal with just one 'yellow Jayhawker lawdog.'

But Jackman was neither yellow nor alone. For as he backed up through wreathing gunsmoke to bring into sight some half-dozen of the enemy with guns in their fists, he cut loose with such ferocity that the clamour sounded like a Gatling, rising above all other sounds.

As bloodied figures tumbled like grisly play-dollies, a bartender crashed an iron across a Texan skull; a gun guard from the stage line snatched up his sawed-off in a near corner and loosed both barrels at McCord's position from close range, and did not miss.

The town was fighting back!

As Johnny Fallon leapt atop the bullet-holed bar he drove two slugs through the back of a Texan rushing the stairs.

A howling figure burst from a side doorway, then turned end over end as he rushed into a withering crossfire. Next instant, Jackman was struck in the shoulder and toppled over a poker layout, yet came up again instantly, still clutching both guns. Windows went out with a tinkling crash and candles, lanterns and chandeliers trembled to the reverberations as the fury continued, the raging fury that was Chisum was suddenly fighting for itself, not for any glorious reason but simply to survive.

As Clay Jackman believed every town should and must . . . not relying on men like him, for surely they were of a vanishing breed. . . .

He triggered and a big-nosed face disappeared in a crimson splatter. Johnny was backing up the staircase to join him and the marshal covered him with shot after shot, each of which found a target. The uproar reached a full-force riot-sized climax which suddenly changed to triumphant cheering when the first blood-spattered Texan waddy hurled himself through a window and took to his heels, signalling the moment in which the battle became a rout.

Down on one knee at a cowboy's side, Jackman brushed the staring eyes shut then calmly gunned down a denim-clad figure in a huge hat and rowel spurs attempting to rush past him to reach a passageway so he might run.

It was his last bullet.

He slumped against a wall and gazed up through the smoke to see a lean figure approaching. He raised his Thuer but didn't trigger as Johnny loomed above him. But this was surely not the Johnny he knew. This was a man with the look which only someone of Jackman's experience could identify at first glance.

It was his own look.

'Just take it easy and I'll clean up, Clay, you've done enough.'

The marshal leaned back with a sigh, head tilted back against the wall as the figure disappeared. He closed his eyes. They didn't need him any longer. Tomorrow a dozen dead men would be quietly awaiting burial, but tonight the flames of Chisum's longest day burned bright.

The chief justice from Capital City had crammed in five days at Chisum with his staff, combing through the turbulent events of the clash between Kansan citizens and Texan trail-drivers. The challenge had seemed like a mountain at first glance, but had been reduced to a molehill by the end of five almost round-the-clock days for the justice, a jury and a helpful citizenry. Today's dismissal of the last Texan witness had signalled the end of the legalities.

The silver-headed trouble-shooter deliberately left the swearing-in ceremony to the last to enable him to leave on a totally positive note.

When it was done, he shook the new marshal's hand warmly and predicted a shining future for him, based on the reports concerning the young man's singular bravery during the riots.

'Congratulations, Marshal Fallon.' He smiled. 'You are certainly the youngest city marshal I've ever sworn in but I have a strong feeling you might well prove one of the finest.' He nodded to Jackman. 'And my best wishes for you in your retirement, Mr Jackman. I hope time will not hang too heavy on your hands.'

Time and its excess or shortage was low on Clay Jackman's list of concerns as the party broke up and they moved out into the sunlight. Nor was he in the slightest concerned that his twenty-year career was finally, officially at an end – or even that Johnny was taking on this heavy responsibility today.

He knew what the boy was capable of; the whole town did and would rally behind him.

But there was an obvious problem.

'I wonder if we should have a shot at the Blue Duck first or head straight for the Lady?' he speculated, lighting a fragrant stogie.

Johnny brushed his shirt-sleeve across his badge and squinted east. 'Flip a coin, Clay?'

'No. Let's be men and face the fire first. It's a good bet we'll need a drink after.'

They sounded sober, and yet that leisurely stroll from jailhouse to saloon in the mild sunshine through a peaceful town was both a tonic and a reward for the two men who had done most to preserve it. The walk helped disperse the tensions, but they were mounting again as they went up the steps of the Painted Lady to be greeted with a big smile from Bowie, who moved smartly to open the batwings for them.

Both looked at the man suspiciously; Bowie was not an easy-smiling man.

They entered the cool gloom of the saloon where drinkers rose to their feet and began singing 'Hail to the Chief!' Tables had been pushed together, there were lighted candles, filled glasses and smiling faces beneath a banner that read:

CONGRATULATIONS MARSHAL FALLON!

The two men turned to stare at one another.

This had to be some kind of weird joke, their expressions said. Carla throwing a party to celebrate her brother's embracing a profession she'd always both feared and hated?

It would be two tantalizing hours before their minds would be set at rest.

Carla made it all sound so simple.

'I only ever saw your work as dangerous and brutal,

156

Clay – I never understood why you had to go out with a gun and kill or be killed. But I'd never seen anything like the horror that erupted here, and I realized – indeed saw with my very own eyes – that but for what you and Johnny did that night, dozens, perhaps scores of innocent people might have perished.'

She paused to glance at her brother, leaning against the rear balcony in the moonlight.

'I realized I'd also been guilty of seeing you still as the boy I'd been left to rear when our folks died. But that night I also realized that if Clay stepped down, Chisum had to have someone just like him to fill his shoes, and you were the only possible choice.'

She smiled brightly, looking from one to the other.

'I think I was the first person in town to recognize that fact, apart from you, Clay. I recognized it, found I could accept it, know now that I'm incredibly proud of what you've become.' Her eyes swung to Jackman. 'What you both are, and will be. . . .'

'Meaning?' Clay said with a smile.

'I think you know what I mean, Clay Jackman,' she said, and opened her arms.

Leaning on the railing, Johnny watched and grinned. Then he used his sleeve to rub up his badge again. Across the room, the stern and often severe face of Clay Jackman looked as if it could not stop smiling.

It was one full week to the day following the riot which had drawn US marshals and officials from as far distant as Dodge and Oklahoma City to investigate, before the mayor's rig eventually returned to Chisum.

Terrified by the prospect of violence, the mayor had

157

fled to his remote hunting-lodge along Singing Creek, out of touch with the world and far from danger until he considered it entirely safe to return.

Chisum's richest citizen showed deep shock at all that met his eyes, and Carter soon found himself obliged to drive around the grocer, silversmith, a farmer from the flats and a couple of junior ranch hands from the Circle W, all of whom refused to make way for his rig, as normally they would.

Sands shot a questioning look at Carter, who spat over a wheel before venturing a reply.

'Looks like we're tainted, you and me, Mayor.'

'Tainted? What kind of foolish talk is that?'

'Read me an article in the Chisum *Herald* up at Pueblo that said they've built up the notion that if you weren't here during the trouble, didn't do your share or risk your neck, then you're like a leper.'

'That's idiotic. I'm their mayor.'

'Another thing I read, but it didn't seem the right time to tell you. They've called for new elections. Cluff's a hot favorite to get elected and they've got you down at odds of ten to one.'

These were stunning blows for Klegg Sands to cope with before he was even properly home, yet he began feeling positive again as they brought the Painted Lady in sight and rolled on up to the front gallery.

Bowie came forward from the batwings but halted on the top step, fists resting on hips, as though barring the entrance. Moments later, Carla appeared from around the corner. She wore a plain dove-grey dress with a high neck and a black calico band round her right upper arm. She looked beautiful.

He felt a surge of optimism. He'd heard about McCord's death and believed his own prospects would have strengthened as a consequence, despite the shadow of his ill-fated posting ordinance. . . .

He jumped down and offered his hand but the woman appeared not to notice.

'Hello, Mr Sands.'

'Hello? Is that all the welcome I get? Carla, there's so much I want to talk about. . . .'

He broke off as the batwings opened outwards. Clay Jackman appeared, wearing eyeglasses and shirtsleeves, leisurely drying a big glass beer-jug with a cotton cloth.

Sands took a full step backwards and Carter gaped. Then Carla ran lightly up the steps to link her arm through Jackman's, leaning her head against his shoulder. 'Meet my new business partner, Mayor Sands. And fiancé.'

'This is loco,' Sands sputtered, staring up at Jackman. 'I heard you'd run . . . where are your guns? You a saloonkeeper? This must be some kind of joke.'

It was no joke. Nor was it any kind of laughing matter when a tall and youthful figure appeared on the porch, the sun glinting off the silver star upon his chest.

Sands's jaw sagged. Johnny Fallon – City Marshal?

Johnny spoke quietly to his sister and Jackman and the party turned and disappeared inside, leaving the porch empty but for the new marshal, Bowie and the grey-faced man of affairs who seemed to have aged years in mere minutes.

But it wasn't over yet. The visiting county officials had carefully investigated all that had happened here over the past month, so Marshal Johnny Fallon informed quietly. The finding was that the mayor's authorization of the posting order against the Pecos herd was illegal and that he would be duly charged and tried for incitement to riot.

The watchers from the windows saw – not a vain and puffed-up pouter-pigeon of a town mayor any longer – but rather a suddenly grey and stiff-jointed old man who eventually clambered back up into his rig for an ashen Carter to drive him away.

Clay glanced down at Carla and marvelled again at the difference a simple pair of spectacles could make to a man's life. For he could see clearly now, looking into her eyes. Saw things which he should have seen a long, long time ago. Saw she had been there just waiting for him all along – waiting patiently for the Gunner to surrender the life he had thought he could not live without, before embracing the real thing.

He kissed her lightly and headed for the bar. There was work to do here that wouldn't wait.